Anonymous

The Life of Samuel P. Godwin

First President of the Godwin Association of the Franklin Reformatory Home for

Inebriates of Philadelphia

Anonymous

The Life of Samuel P. Godwin
First President of the Godwin Association of the Franklin Reformatory Home for Inebriates of Philadelphia

ISBN/EAN: 9783337297596

Printed in Europe, USA, Canada, Australia, Japan

Cover: Foto ©Raphael Reischuk / pixelio.de

More available books at **www.hansebooks.com**

THE LIFE

OF

SAMUEL P. GODWIN,

FIRST PRESIDENT

OF THE

GODWIN ASSOCIATION

OF THE

Franklin Reformatory Home for Inebriates

OF

PHILADELPHIA.

———

PHILADELPHIA:
TREAGER & LAMB, PRINTERS AND PUBLISHERS,
No. 32 South Seventh Street,
1889.

In Memoriam.

Samuel Paynter Godwin.

FIRST PRESIDENT,

(1872-1889)

OF THE

FRANKLIN REFORMATORY HOME,

OF

PHILADELPHIA,

FOUNDED APRIL 1ST, 1872.

AND

FIRST PRESIDENT,

(1872-1889)

OF THE

GODWIN ASSOCIATION

OF THE

FRANKLIN REFORMATORY HOME,

FOUNDED JUNE 20TH, 1872.

BORN, OCTOBER 16TH, 1825,

ENTERED INTO REST, FEBRUARY 17TH, 1889.

TO
THE MEMBERS
OF
THE GODWIN ASSOCIATION
OF THE
FRANKLIN REFORMATORY HOME
FOR INEBRIATES
OF
PHILADELPHIA,

This sketch of the Life of their late beloved FIRST PRESIDENT, prepared at their request, is respectfully dedicated by their Committee on Records.

C. J. GIBBONS, *Chairman.*
E. G. PRICE,
ROBT. MOFFAT.

PREAMBLE AND RESOLUTION.

At a meeting of the Godwin Association of the Franklin Home, held on February 21st, 1889, the following Preamble and Resolution were offered by Mr. C. J. Gibbons, and unanimously adopted :

"The Members of the Godwin Association of the Franklin Home, having regard to the great loss sustained, by their body, in the death of their beloved President, Mr. Samuel P. Godwin, feeling how very greatly his teaching and influence will be missed by each individual member, as well as by the Association as a whole, and appreciating, as they do, the value of his loving example and kindly counsels,

"*Resolve*, That the Committee on Records be requested to prepare a History of this Association, as connected with the life of the late President, not in a spirit of laudation of the man who was its founder, its earnest teacher, and its wise counsellor, who may well be said to have laid down his life for its members (for his life, devoted to God, and through God to his fellow-men, needs not the praise of men) ; but that they may possess for themselves, may preserve and hand down that History to the men who, in the future, will become members of the Association, thus affording an example for their lives, and a beacon-light for the great cause in which Mr. Godwin labored with such energy and zeal."

CONTENTS.

IN MEMORIAM.
SAMUEL P. GODWIN.

Died February 17th, 1889.

"Be thou faithful unto death, and I will give thee a crown of life."—Rev. ii : 10.

"Blessed is the man that endureth temptation; for when he is tried, he shall receive the crown of life, which the Lord has promised to them that love Him."—James i : 12.

"Henceforth there is laid up for me a crown of righteousness, which the Lord, the righteous Judge, shall give me at that day."—2 Tim. iv : 8.

Out of the dreams of an earthly sleep,
    Into the light of a Sabbath day,
A Sabbath that hath no setting sun,
    Where holy joys pass not away;
Opening his eyes with rapturous gaze,
    Out of the darkness into the light,
Looking up to his Saviour's face,
    No veil between to dim the sight.

Into his soul made pure and white,
    Rejoicing and free from sin's fell power,
There came the words he had craved so oft
    Deep in his heart in some prayerful hour:
"Servant, well done, thou hast fought the fight,
    Shrinking not from its weary strife;
Enter thou into the joy of thy Lord;
    For thee is waiting a crown of life."

Ye who know how he loved the Lord,
 Pleading so oft God's love to you,
Pointing the way to the crucified;
 Was he not always faithful and true?
Ye who have felt the clasp of his hand,
 Strong as the pity and love he gave;
Hear ye not still his pleading voice
 Telling of Him who is mighty to save?

To snatch men out of the depths of sin,
 To tell how manhood they could regain,
To cheer the sad, the wavering to hold;
 His noble life was not in vain.
Though death came with a sudden stroke,
 For him the victory was won:
In Jesus' name, we bow and say,
 God knoweth best: his work was done.

Gone to the life of the purified,
 Into the land of the saved and the blest,
Into the home for him prepared,
 Into the peace of perfect rest;
Gone from among you, just gone before,
 Beckoning you still with a loving hand,
Pointing to Jesus, your only hope,
 Your only guide to that Heavenly Land.
     Faith Holden.

INTRODUCTION.

" I hold it truth with him who sings
To one clear harp in divers tones,
That men may rise on stepping stones
Of their dead selves to higher things."

TENNYSON.

Among the many vices which stain and disfigure man, who was created in the likeness of God, none is more destructive in its temporal and eternal effects than Intemperance. Physiologists warn us, daily experience tells us that it destroys the powers of mind and body. The great Apostle of the Gentiles declares to us that "drunkards" "shall not inherit the kingdom of God."

Just as surely as the drunkard's death awaits the man who persists in his vice, does alienation from the light of God overtake him who is not raised, by mercy and grace, from the slough of sin and shame into which intemperance plunges him.

Actuated by such considerations, in the warfare against this subtle enemy of the body and soul of man, some noble spirits have forged to the front, holding on high their standard of hope, before the eyes of the world ; and others, more content with the sphere of work with which God has environed them, in none the less heroic manner have fought a good fight, inspired by faith in God's love, power and promises, by hope in God's mercy towards the men of His creation, and by charity to those who have fallen under the tempter's snare.

The subject of the following sketch, the guide and leader of the Association at whose request this history is prepared, was one of the latter. Content, amid the daily business of an active city life, to take the work which lay around him, he put his hand to the plough and did his task with all his might.

Of the magnitude of that work the reader of these pages must judge. It will be sufficient to say that many who have been turned to righteousness by the bright example, fervid teaching, loving assistance and ennobling influence of the First President of the Godwin Association of Philadelphia, feel that they have reason to take to heart the words of their Divine Master, "For what is a man profited if he gain the whole world and lose his own soul? or what shall a man give in exchange for his soul?" Estimated in accordance with such a standard, the fruits of Mr. Godwin's labors are priceless, and such will ever be the value placed upon them by those who are a living monument to his self-sacrifice and zeal.

But these pages are not intended as mere praise of one who, in his humility, deprecated even the slightest acknowledgment of his work ; whose delight it was ever to remain in the back-ground and allow the honor of success to fall on others. They are intended to be a record which will always be treasured up by those who derived benefit, hope, reformation and restoration from their intercourse with him. They are intended to be a legacy which such men may leave to those who come after them. They are intended to be a guide to such men themselves in their earthly life, an example to the world around, re-echoing the command of Him who loved us :—

"Go and do thou likewise."

A SKETCH OF
SAMUEL P. GODWIN'S LIFE.

" Lives of great men all remind us,
We may make our lives sublime,
And departing leave behind us
Footprints on the sands of time :

Footprints that perchance another,
Sailing o'er life's solemn main,
A forlorn and shipwrecked brother,
Seeing may take heart again."

LONGFELLOW.

Samuel Paynter Godwin was a native of the State of Delaware, being born at Milford, on October 16th, 1825. His father, the Rev. Daniel Godwin, was born on August 24th, 1774, and was for more than fifty years a local preacher of the Methodist Church. It is recorded of him that "he was a man of genial, Christian character, and widely known and respected, having during a long life won and retained the high appreciation of a large circle of friends." He died at Milford, on March 5th, 1866, in the ninety-second year of age.

Mr. Godwin's grandfather was born in Maryland, and came from Talbot county to Delaware, early in life.

His mother was Elizabeth, daughter of Nehemiah and Rachel Davis, of Prime Hook, who were among the early Methodists of Delaware. She was born on March 15th, 1786, and died, in the same year as her husband, on November 10th, 1866, in the eighty-first year of her age.

Under the Christian influence of such parents, those foundations of faith, hope and charity were firmly laid, which stood Samuel P. Godwin in good stead in his early life, and formed the basis on which he built up that strength of character and Christ-like devotion to duty which marked his life of activity, as well as his philanthropic efforts for the benefit of humanity.

He was educated at the old Masonic

Academy in Milford, under the Rev. Orin R. Howard and Alfred Emerson ; but when most youths of the present generation may be said to be beginning the real work of education, he left the academy to plunge into the whirl of a business life— a fact which is astonishing to all those who realized, in the days of his manhood, the extent of the field of his knowledge and his intellectual attainments.

At the early age of twelve years, he was sent to Philadelphia to begin business life in the store of McNeil & Moore, of No. 23 N. Third Street, where he remained four years, until the firm retired from business. He was then sixteen years of age, and became a book-keeper in the firm of Vogel & Virden, holding this post until 1848.

He had been in Philadelphia during the most trying period of life— the period of the development of the boy into the man. To all who know the temptations of a city

life at this impressionable crisis, it cannot
appear other than providential that he
came out of the ordeal unscathed, sustained by the teachings of his childhood
and boyhood ; and he could not have been
fitted in a more effectual way for the work
in which he afterwards labored so earnestly—the rescuing of ·his fellowmen from
temptation and the reformation of those
who had not found strength to resist it.
He exemplified, in every respect, the poet's
words :

> " My strength is as the strength of ten,
>   Because my heart is pure."

In 1848, he returned to his native town
and entered into business as partner with
his father and elder brother, Mr. Daniel
Godwin, under the name of Godwin & Co.
While here, he became a member of the
Order of Odd Fellows, and the brethren,
recognizing the value of his business capacities, as well as his sterling worth and

ability, elected him to the several chairs in succession; until he held the honorable position of Deputy Grand Master of the State of Delaware. Well did he in after years carry out the great principles of the Order in brotherhood, benevolence, purity, truth and charity.

The same spirit, doubtless, made him join the Masonic Order; and he was admitted into the Temple Lodge of Ancient York Masons, at Milford.

Preferring a wider business sphere, he returned to Philadelphia in the spring of 1851, and until 1857, was connected with Hamman, Snyder & Co., whom he left to enter the house of Atwood & Co. Previous to this, like a loving, true and affectionate son, as he ever was, he purchased a house at Milford, in which he placed his father and mother, thus providing them with every possible comfort during the sunset of their lives.

Leaving Atwood & Co. in the autumn

of 1861, he became a partner in the oldest
wholesale dry goods house in Philadelphia,
then known as Wood, Marsh, Hayward &
Co., afterwards as Wood, Marsh & Co.,
and still later as Wood, Bacon & Co.   He
remained a member of this firm for twenty-
three years.   On January 1st, 1886, he
undertook a responsible post with Hood,
Bonbright & Co., and when the business
of that firm passed into the hands of Mr.
John Wanamaker, in February, 1888, he
still remained identified with' it, and continued so until his death, in February,
1889.

On December 16th, 1857, in Grace Protestant Episcopal Church, at Philadelphia,
Mr. Godwin married Miss Emma G.,
daughter of the late John Eisenbrey, Esq.,
of Philadelphia ; and two children were
born of the marriage, Anna E. and William Harrison Godwin.

Into the sacred recesses of a private
life, known only to the inner circle of de-

voted friends, it is not the concern, as it is
not the purpose, of this memoir to pene-
trate. But it could not escape the notice
of even the most casual observer, that intense mutual love reigned supreme in all
his family relations ; and his habit of greeting his wife and children with warm affection, on leaving, or returning to his home,
was remarkable. Strikingly characteristic,
also, were the simplicity and purity which
pervaded the very atmosphere, making
that home the recipient of God's blessing
and worthy of man's highest venera-
tion. There Mr. Godwin's memory is
treasured up with a love which will ever
surround his name with that halo of sanc-
tity which is the glory of an irreproachable
life. The trite expressions, "an affectionate father, husband, friend," go a very
little way towards describing his character.
Rather would we employ the words of
one who knew him in his most intimate

relations: "How little we knew what a saint we had in the family!"

Recognized in business circles as a man of great ability, he was even better and more widely known as one who devoted every available moment to works of philanthropy. Eager as he was to promote the welfare of humanity, he, at an early age, threw all the weight of his Christian principles, his strength of character and his innate liberality into the work of assisting the poor and the outcast and instructing the ignorant.

Those who conversed with him, even in his early life, discovered that generous disposition and impetuous nature which maturer years and experience in the world, coupled with God's grace, developed into that Christ-like charity which knew no sect, no nationality, in its object, but saw a brother in every sufferer and fallen man.

He found, to a certain extent, an outlet for his energies and his philanthropy in

what might be called general Temperance
work, to which he was ever earnestly attached; but it was as an active Christian
worker for and in the Church that he
showed, on every occasion and opportunity, those beautiful traits of character with
which God had endowed him, and which
marked him as a leader among leaders.

It will be worth while to trace, for a
little space, the work which gave him that
experience which so eminently fitted him
to be the Christian teacher of the men
who fell under his influence during the last
seventeen years of his life.

He associated himself with nearly every
Temperance organization of Philadelphia,
especially the American Temperance
Union, the Sons of Temperance, and the
Good Templars. He became a Vice-
President of the Bedford Street Mission,
of the Society for Preventing the Sunday
Liquor Traffic and the Society for Pre-
venting Cruelty to Children. Doubtless, in

his intercourse with those with whom he was, in this way, brought in contact, he gained a knowledge of that degradation which is the result of vice; but which the stratum of society in which he naturally moved too often pushes out of sight, or passes by in the pomp of pride, with the feeling:—"Stand by, I am holier than thou."

Mr. Godwin had been trained, as before stated, in the strict school of the early Methodists of Delaware. When twelve years of age he joined the Methodist Episcopal Church of his native town, showing, while yet so young, how deeply the associations and teachings of his childhood and boyhood had sunk into his heart.

On coming to Philadelphia in 1851, he became a member of the Bible Class conducted by Mr. Solomon Townsend, in connection with the Union Methodist Episcopal Church, Fourth Street.

In 1859 his convictions led him to associate himself with St. Andrew's Protestant Episcopal Church, and his affectionate friend and co-laborer, Mr. Frederick Scofield, thus speaks of his work there :—

"Mr. S. P. Godwin, on becoming a member of the congregation of St. Andrew's Church, was told by the Rector, the Rev. W. F. Paddock, D. D., to visit the different Sunday Schools connected with the church, and see where he could be most useful. He came to the Sunday School held at the Mission Chapel of St. Andrew's Church, on Thirteenth Street below Washington Avenue, introduced himself to the Superintendent—myself—and said, 'At the request of the Rector, I have visited the different schools (some three) connected with the church, and this is the last. I am much pleased with this school and its surroundings ; it seems to be the place for me. If you will give me a class, I will throw my lot in with you.'

"Most gladly a class was given him. He

proved to be a most faithful and efficient
teacher, and very soon gained the love
and respect of his scholars.   He was ever
ready to enter into anything, however
difficult, for the good of the school and
the welfare of the scholars, or to contribute
to the support of the school ; and, as Superintendent, I owed much to him for aid and
wise counsels in carrying out the work.
A warm friendship grew up between us,
which has never abated.   For some nine
years, we two would travel together from
Eighth and Spruce Streets to Thirteenth
and Washington Avenue and back again
on each Sunday afternoon.   Mr. Godwin
was never absent, unless out of the city,
or in consequence of something over which
he had no control.

"In 1869, the chapel had grown into a
Church organization, and the school was
handed over to the Church of the Messiah,
which afterwards removed to its new build-

ing at the corner of Broad and Federal streets.

In the fall of 1868, the Rector of St. Andrew's Church, the Rev. W. F. Paddock, D. D., requested Mr. Godwin to take charge of the Young Men's Bible Class held on Sunday morning in the Vestry room of the church. The class, at this time, was quite small; but by prayer, faith, great energy, and making the study of the Bible a pleasant study, it increased until it numbered some two hundred members. Every Sunday morning, the room was crowded with young men engaged in the study of God's Holy Word, drinking in the precious truths instilled into their minds by their teacher. What the harvest of the good seed thus sown will be, eternity alone can reveal."

The value of Mr. Godwin's work in the congregation of St. Andrew's may be gathered from the fact that it received Episcopal sanction; Mr. Godwin being

3

licensed, as a Lay Reader, by Bishop Stevens. Among the papers highly prized by his family is the following:

" DIOCESE OF PENNSYLVANIA,
" EPISCOPAL ROOMS, 708 Walnut St.,
"PHILADELPHIA, June 18, 1873.

" Mr. S. P. Godwin is hereby licensed to officiate as a Lay Reader under the direction of the Rev. W. F. Paddock, D. D., Mr. Godwin promising to observe and comply with the provisions of the Canon on Lay Readers in the Digest.
"WM. BACON STEVENS,
" *Bp. of the Dio. of Penna.*"

But the fullest, most interesting and most valuable account of Mr. Godwin's work at St. Andrew's Church will be found in the subjoined letter received from his friend, the Rev. W. F. Paddock, D. D., by Mr. F. Scofield, who at the time of Mr. Godwin's death was the Chairman of the Executive Committee of the Franklin

Home, and has now succeeded him in the Presidency of the Institution :

"EARLY CHRISTIAN LIFE AND CHURCH WORK.

"When the distinguished Methodist divine and pulpit orator, John Summerfield, once was asked where he was born, he replied: "I was born in England, and born again in Ireland." The change wrought in his moral nature at his conversion was so deep and radical he could apply to it no other than the Scriptural term, a new birth. In England he had his natural birth, in Ireland his spiritual.

"In St. Andrew's Church, Philadelphia, Samuel P. Godwin, though the subject of strong religious convictions, and actually connected with another Church from his boyhood, first became, in a public manner, a member of the Protestant Episcopal Church. It was no slight change which then took place in his heart and life, no transient effect of over-excited feeling, no mere external and surface work. There was rather a transformation of his former self, a re-creation, by the Divine Spirit, of the whole man in righteousness and true holiness. As his pastor, I joyfully marked the various stages of this development of spiritual life, and when, on the 4th of June, 1865, he came forward to publicly proclaim in the Rite of Confirmation his renunciation of the world, and love and dependence upon Christ, the assurance was strong and abiding that it was no empty profession, but a real, thorough, life-long dedication of himself to God. It was an added gratification that the taking of this step was in hearty accord with the preference and convictions of a faithful wife who, inspired by the devout conduct of her husband, at the same chancel, assumed like vows of discipleship. Thus were they united not only in kindred service and devotion, but by ties of sacred affection which death could not sever.

"Having put on the Christian armor, Mr. Godwin immediately entered the field to fight for Christ and His Truth. He loved not inaction, when anything needed to be done—to lie ingloriously in his tent when

the enemy was abroad. The missionary
work of the Church, and the enlargement
of its Sunday Schools and Bible Classes,
first engaged his attention. St. Andrew's
Mission on South Thirteenth Street—since
grown into a Church organization under
the name of the Church of the Messiah—
was then deeply interesting the workers
of the parent Church, and was the centre
of their activity. From small beginnings,
under the able Superintendency of Mr.
Frederick Scofield, the Sunday School had
gathered in nearly three hundred children ;
the Chapel was filled, morning and evening, with attentive congregations; and the
whole surrounding population were in a
marked degree morally and materially
improved. Into this missionary enterprise
Mr. Godwin threw himself with his usual
energy, lending voice, influence, means, to
its wisely directed operations. He took
the deepest interest in every new plan
and project for its advancement. He loved
the Gospel there preached and taught,
and the souls of those who heard it. He
rejoiced in the outward prosperity and

success attending the work, but above all
in the many souls won to Christ, and in
the elevating and morally beneficent influence the Mission exercised upon the
neighborhood.

"In October, 1869, he started the afterwards famous Young Men's Bible Class
of St. Andrew's Church. Only one scholar
was present at its first session. In seven
months sixty members were enrolled. As
the years went by, this number was increased to one hundred, and then to one
hundred and fifty, and finally to nearly two
hundred. The young men were drawn
from all denominations, all avocations, all
parts of the city. And yet such was the
tact and large-hearted Catholicity of their
teacher, that denominational lines and pre-
ferences were scarcely thought of, and
never disagreeably prominent, and social
grades and extraneous advantages were
unrecognized and unregarded. He taught
them that in the Church of Christ all were
one; and exemplified in his practice this
teaching.

"Courtesy was a distinguishing feature

of the Class; not only between teachers
and scholars, but between scholar and
scholar, and between both and the pastor.
The teacher always announced the pastor's entrance into the Class-room, and
then all arose to pay him respect. When
seated, the subject of the lesson was mentioned, in order that the pastor might sustain previous instruction by his testimony,
and give to it increased interest and
variety.

"The instruction was always given in
the form of lectures, carefully prepared
and effectively delivered. 'I will not render unto God that which costs me nothing,'
was Mr. Godwin's motto in all he did;
and it was a matter of surprise how he
could find time, with the varied demands
and harassing cares of his large mercan-
tile operations and the claims of social
and domestic life, to furnish, each week,
profitable and well-digested instruction
drawn from such wide fields of observation
and research. While he read much, his
lectures could not be called learned or
profound. Rather were they plain expo-

sitions of Bible Truths, illustrated by familiar facts and everyday experiences, and confirmed by the testimony of distinguished writers and Christian workers. Avoiding wearisome theological disquisitions, and clothing what he said with present practical interest, the members of his class found, not only moral improvement, but intellectual recreation in the Class-room; and attendance upon its sessions became an enjoyable duty rather than an irksome task. This, with the enthusiasm he inspired in Bible study and the missionary zeal he invoked and directed, together with his unceasing prayer for Divine aid, and assured belief in the value and potency of Divine truth, made his Bible Class the success it was, both in its membership and moral and religious results.

" Mr. Godwin's witness and labors were not confined to work among young men. He deeply loved and earnestly sought to promote the prosperity of the Church that had been instrumental in widening and deepening his walk with Christ. He was regular in attendance upon its services,

liberal in his contributions to its support,
unwearied in his efforts to increase its
spirituality, and enlarge its membership
and extend its influence. Soon after his
confirmation, being elected a member of its
Vestry, he introduced into that body various measures for extending and perfect-
ing its work and perpetuating its usefulness. The project of raising a large En-
dowment Fund—suggested by the late
Arthur G. Coffin—secured his hearty approval and generous support. He was
the chairman of the committee that issued
the Appeal of 1871, setting forth the imperative need and solemn duty of making
liberal provision for the future of this his-
toric Church, and was prominent in devising and carrying out plans for its accom-
plishment. He took an active part also
in the Semi-Centennial celebration of St.
Andrew's, in 1873, being chairman of two
of the committees, and a member of two
others, engaged in organizing and bringing
to a successful termination the most important and interesting week of services
ever held in the Church.

"But valuable and many as were his services for Christ and humanity, by far his greatest work, his crowning achievement, and that which will ever remain his truest monument is, 'The Franklin Reformatory Home.' The plan was sketched and the foundations were laid while he was a vestryman of St. Andrew's Church, and in laying them broad and deep he received the efficient aid and moral support of its officers and members, some of whom are still actively connected with the institution.

"Of Mr. Godwin's work for the inebriate, others are more competent to speak than myself. I may, however, say that the principles upon which it was based, viz.: 'that conversion is necessary to permanent reformation ; and that the power of man is helpless without the grace of God,' are of supreme value and ever to be remembered, in all efforts to exalt the race ; and never more so than in trying to save the inebriate. 'Not by might, nor by power, but by my Spirit, saith the Lord of Hosts.'"

Mr. Godwin's interest, however, was

not bounded by the circle of St. Andrew's. He gladly gave whatever assistance he could to the humbler churches of the city, and in none did he work more effectively than in those of the colored people, among whom he will long be remembered with affection and esteem. As evidence of this, it may be stated that he was a Vestryman of the Church of the Crucifixion, and a Trustee of the Home for the Homeless in connection with that Church.

His own feelings with regard to the colored race were very pronounced. In 1872 he publicly said to them:

" Your brethren are no longer bound with the chains of the mercenary demon; they are now at liberty, through the justice and mercy of God; you all then have a right, an indisputable right, to aspire to equality. The same God who made you made me, the same free gift of salvation is as well yours as mine, and the same heaven of happiness, in the bright and glorious future which has been secured to

me, is alike your own.   John the Divine
tells you, 'there is no night there;' I say
to you there is no caste there.   God, your
Father and my Father reigns supreme in
that blessed mansion, and knows no distinction among His children, save as their
good works merit a higher reward.   God
is no respecter of persons; Jew or Gentile,
bond or free, white or colored, are indis-
solubly one in Heaven, for they are all
the offspring of the one common parent.
Would you have a foretaste of that home
of happiness, while on earth? then discharge the duty of the hour."

And again :—" What a glorious day for
yourselves, what a glorious day for the true,
tried and zealous friends of your race, will
that be when the world shall be convinced
that the colored race is eminently fitted to
fill the bar, the pulpit, the rostrum, and
society, with talent and respectability, un-
surpassed and unsurpassable!"

The following letter from Mr. W. Still,
himself well known for his generous
philanthropy among his own race of the

colored people, will afford fitting evidence of the warmth of affection with which Mr. Godwin worked when opportunity served:

"MARCH 23, 1889.

" MR. C. J. GIBBONS,

"DEAR SIR:—Hearing that the friends of the late Samuel P. Godwin are preparing a sketch of his life and works, it occurred to me that I might be excused for adding a very brief tribute on this occasion.

"A very warm and cordial friendship existed between Mr. Godwin and myself for more than a score of years, and I always found him one of the most faithful and unswerving friends of Freedom, and by his death I feel that I have been deprived of a great personal friend.

"It was my good fortune to make his acquaintance, for the first time, sometime during the late Rebellion, when the colored people here, as indeed everywhere in this land, were greatly agitated over the war and the prospect of Freedom, and needed much wise counsel and friendly encouragement.

"I can recall no other individual of the Anglo-Saxon race, lay or clerical, who, in this dark hour, appeared more frequently among the colored people in their various churches and assemblies, than Samuel P. Godwin, who always showed the most ardent interest in their spiritual, moral and temporal advancement.

"Although a staunch Episcopalian, his Church relations, as such, never seemed to debar him from affiliating with other religious denominations, wherever and whenever his services seemed to be required to uphold true Christianity and the just rights of man.

"He was no 'sectarian.' He sympathized especially with the poor, oppressed and degraded classes in society, without regard to race or color.

"Of course, his idea of living as a disciple of Christ led him to oppose with all his might, whenever opportunity offered, the degrading drink and saloon curse, and it was apparent that his labors were not without effect.

"Doubtless the light he discovered in

searching out wrong and battling against
it, in those earlier days to which I have
referred, greatly strengthened and prepared him for the wider field of labor that
he entered upon in helping to establish
'The Franklin Reformatory Home,' to
which so many of the later years of his
assiduous labors were devoted.

"However, it is not necessary, that I
should further allude to his labors in this
charity, or indeed in any of the other
philanthropic charitable institutions, where
he was so frequently called upon to labor
for the elevation of mankind.

"But I cannot forego the opportunity of
briefly remarking how heartily he sympathized with 'The Home for Aged and Infirm Colored Persons,' and how much he
delighted to visit its inmates on religious
and other errands, in order to serve them.
For a number of years he was quite a frequent visitor on Sabbath days, and I think
I am safe in saying that the old people
never seemed better pleased, never seemed
to manifest greater appreciation, never
seemed to be inspired with more gratitude

to God and good friends, than when in his
presence, and under his enthusiastic preach-
ing and sympathy.

"Often he would say to me, that there
was no place where he visited—churches
or institutions—where he derived so much
enjoyment and spiritual comfort, as at
'The Home for Aged and Infirm Colored
Persons.'

"Mr. Godwin seemed to understand the
old people thoroughly, and he treated them
as though he believed they fully understood him. In speaking he would often
allude to his boyhood days, when in the
State of Delaware, in the days of slavery,
he came much in contact with colored
people and especially certain aged ones
who, by some attentions to him, had always
made him remember them gratefully. And
as he could go back to his young manhood
days, and there date his abhorrence of
slavery and his love of freedom and sympathy for the colored people, he seemed
doubly qualified to impress them with his
friendship.

"I like so well to think of Mr. Godwin as

a worker and a friend, meeting, as we did, on various occasions at the Home, and of the interesting incidents which would occasionally occur, that it would not be difficult for me to extend this letter to an undue length. A single incident, however, must suffice for the present: A year or two ago, Mr. Godwin was at the Home, by invitation. Signs of failing health were very apparent and I could not suppress my fears with regard to the unfavorable indications, and said to him, 'your incessant labors, and overtaxation will surely kill you,' and I further remarked that 'you would be much oftener invited to the 'Home,' if it did not seem like unkindness to impose upon one so generous hearted.' He told me that when he arose in the morning he did not feel at all well, and was doubtful whether he would be able to come; but in speaking to his wife he said that he had promised and he must fulfil his engagement to me to be with the old people at the Home. So he was there.

"Fortunately, that morning, a young woman from the South, who had been

laboring as a missionary among the poorest of the freed children and the most
helpless among the aged and infirm, was
also present; and as she was on her way
to be a missionary in the Congo Valley, it
was thought desirable to hear her, with
regard to the work in which she had been
engaged in Florida, as well as with regard
to the motives which had led her to quit
that needy field and to turn her steps to
the Dark Continent, thousands of miles
away.

"The young woman's name was Miss
Fleming, educated at Shaw University, N.
C., where she took the first rank in her
class.

"She readily assented to give some statement of her work in Florida, and the
reason of her going to the Congo Valley. Modestly, but in most pathetic and
beautiful language, she portrayed the
status of the people among whom she
had labored, and it was apparent enough
that they stood much in need of just
such an intelligent and devoted Christian
woman as herself in their midst; never-

theless to my great surprise, as well as to the surprise of all present, she satisfied us all, that it was her undoubted duty to make the sacrifice of home, friends and everything, and go and labor among the heathen. Every word she uttered seemed to force tears from every eye and completely captivated her hearers.

"At the close of her remarks Mr. Godwin arose. His feelings of sickness having all subsided, he expressed his great thankfulness for being able to be present, and spoke of the relief which had come to his mind from what he had heard, and of the great lesson it ought to prove. He then went on to make the most eloquent and earnest appeal in behalf of the wronged ones in the South, and the heathen in the Congo Valley, to which it had ever been my privilege to listen. And in his utterances he proferred liberal pecuniary aid and whatever influence he could command to help to further the cause of the mission.

"I have witnessed many interesting occasions at the Home in which Mr. Godwin has been a participant, but none equal to

this, and I am fully persuaded that the profound impression made on all present can
never be forgotten.

"I am, yours respectfully,
"WILLIAM STILL."

Mr. Godwin also found time among his
many engagements to visit Girard College,
and the President of that Institution, A. H.
Fetterolf, Ph. D., says: "Mr. Godwin was
one of our most acceptable speakers. He
was earnest and discreet, and always held
the attention of his hearers. His love for
young people, and his great interest in
young men starting in life, showed themselves in everything he did and said. The
boys of the College all felt that they had
a friend in Mr. Godwin. In his death I
realize that I have lost a good friend."

Later on in his life, Mr. Godwin became
warmly attached to the Church of the
Epiphany, and the tribute paid to his
memory by the Rector, the Rev. G. H.
Kinsolving, at the funeral, bore testimony

to the love and respect he had gained in the hearts of the congregation.

In all that has thus far been recorded the spirit of the man is apparent. Every act of his life was guided by the principles of his Christian faith, which to him was not the narrow thing many who profess it would have it be—a bridge by which they, themselves, wrapped in their robe of self-righteousness, may safely pass the dark valley of the shadows; but a Faith which inculcates that Divine Law of universal charity—" Whatsoever ye would that men should do unto you even so do unto them."

THE BIBLE CLASS.

---

*" Wherewithal shall a young man cleanse his way ?
by taking heed thereto according to Thy word."—*
Psalm cxix : 9.

On October 3d, 1869, Mr. Godwin took
charge of the Bible Class at St. Andrew's
Church, referred to by Dr. Paddock and
Mr. Scofield. The following extract from
a journal of the Class, kept by him, shows
the spirit in which he began his work :

"At the solicitation of the Rector of St.
Andrew's P. E. Church, the Rev. W. F.
Paddock, D. D., and after due delibera-
tion, and earnest prayer, I assumed the
Superintendence of 'The Young Men's
Bible Class.' The session commenced
this day at 9 A. M. Through a pouring
rain I went to the Church, and took the
third story back room of the Chapel.
There was but one scholar present, viz.,
C. C. He and I passed the hour very

pleasantly. Dr. Paddock came up, and was introduced to Mr. C. I concluded not to go into a regular organization, until the following Sabbath.

"God grant me the strength and ability to impress upon these young men the necessity of living *very near* to the Cross of Christ."

On the following Sunday, Mr. Godwin recorded :

"Another wet and disagreeable day. I was at my post in the Vestry Room (having changed to that room) at 9 o'clock, and was cheered by the presence of five young men. I spent the hour very agreeably, and, I think, profitably ; and we were visited by Dr. Paddock and James W. Hazlehurst. Dr. P. gave us a few words of encouragement and left. I was much pleased with the strict attention the Class gave to my Introductory, especially that portion of it which related to some of the outside features of the Bible.

" Precious Saviour, assist me to say something to these young men that may be of lasting benefit. Without Thy aid I cannot accomplish any good. O God grant my heart's desire for Christ's sake."

The Class rapidly increased in numbers under Mr. Godwin, until it became an organization of great utility, active in Church and Missionary work. As soon as Mr. Godwin undertook the post of Superintendent, he began to interest the young men in the cause of missions, and in one year, $76.15 were subscribed. In this work, as in all others, he, first of all, laid down a plan for his own guidance, and gradually developed his scheme towards completion, resting not until he had realized his idea. Fortunately for those who may hereafter be engaged in a similar duty, and into whose hands this record of his life may fall, his "Introductory" has been preserved, and is here reproduced, as he himself prepared it :

"In commencing this work for God, and for the mutual instruction and benefit of each other, it will be our heartfelt desire to make the lessons as interesting, instruc-

tive and beneficial as is within our power,
looking unto the Author of every good
and perfect gift for assistance to this end.
We purpose to vary the exercises from
week to week, in the following manner,
viz. : The first Sunday in the month, a
lecture, or recitation, by the Superintendent ; the second Sunday, a lesson from the
Old Testament ; the third Sunday, a lesson
from the New Testament ; the fourth Sunday, an essay on Bible History, by some
member of the Class, together with conversation upon religious subjects. When
there are five Sundays in the month, the
fifth will be assigned to a lesson from the
New Testament. It is our intention to
adopt this course, in order that whilst we
are interested in the exercises, we may
also be stirred up to stricter application
by the variety.

"We are here, my dear scholars, for
the purpose of imparting and receiving
Scriptural knowledge. We are here for
the purpose of doing good and getting
good. Your Superintendent expects to
be as much benefitted as yourselves, and,

oh, how delightful the retrospection, when you and I shall have reached old age, to think that we have associated together in pleasant fellowship to talk of Jesus, to learn more about our precious Saviour, and to become more familiar with the inspired Word of God. Let us, then, see with eye to eye, having but 'one Lord, one faith, one baptism.' Let us use our best endeavors to advance the kingdom of Christ.

" Most of us are mixed up with the cares, vexations and annoyances of business life, are surrounded with those bad influences which are hard to withstand. We need, therefore, such an assembling together of ourselves on the Lord's Day, to be fitted for the journey of life and protected from sin's contamination. It is not right, it is not profitable, it is a sin, to devote all our time and energies to the world ; not being willing to devote one hour to delightful, refreshing, beneficial conversation concerning our Creator, Preserver, and Benefactor.

" We are now going to pledge ourselves to do something for Him who has done so

much for us ; we are going to do our very
best towards strengthening the good resolves of each other, towards reaching out
for a knowledge of godliness, which is far
better than gold, rubies, or precious stones;
towards realizing the fact of the inspired
word of Daniel, the prophet, that : 'They
that be wise shall shine as the firmament,
and they that turn many to righteousness
as the stars for ever and ever.'

" This is a delightful work, it leaves no
sting of conscience, it yields inexpressible
pleasure. We will enter into it, fully resolved to discharge, as far as in us lies,
our duty to our God, ourselves, and our
fellow-man. 'His ways are ways of pleasantness and all His paths are peace.' We
will run to do the works of our Master,
by giving heed to the instructions we receive from His Holy Word, and by showing our appreciation of this privilege by
regular attendance and strict attention.

" These are, I sincerely believe, our de-
cided intentions, and although as sincere
as truth itself, yet not within the power of
self-resolve, unless aided by the all-power-

ful help of God. 'Paul may plant and Apollos may water, but God giveth the increase.' It is earnest, faithful, devoted prayer to that invisible Power, which never deceives, which will give us strength and ability to perform those things which we most desire. There is efficacy in prayer, and God will hear and answer our petitions, if we have faith to believe it; and we can do that which we desire, and more too, if we ask assistance and believe that we shall receive it.

"Let us, then, my dear young friends, being one household of fa'th, and one family of prayer, work earnestly, steadily together, to learn more of our Master and His works than we have ever yet known. We have no personal ends to subserve, no worldly gain to amass in these social gatherings, where we come to learn of God; but our present, future and eternal welfare depends upon the knowledge we gain and the end to which we apply it. Each one of us needs all the information we can derive from the Word of God, in order to stem the torrent of wickedness,

which is flooding every thoroughfare of
life. We must know more about Jesus to
ask His protection; we must live nearer
the Cross, if we expect to feel the efficacy
of its power; we must 'be up and doing'
'whilst it is called day,' lest the night of
death overtakes us.

"We can make these lessons deeply,
yea, intensely interesting, if we but put
our shoulders to the wheel in real earnest,
and we shall have reason to thank God
that we ever met in this Bible Class Room.

"Your Superintendent feels his own
weakness, his utter incapacity to instruct
in Divine things, unless you unite with
him in asking and claiming the blessing of
God. United, as with one heart, we can
and will be delighted to be found together.
'A House divided against itself' must fall.
Come with him, then, to the feet of Jesus,
in your quiet chamber, and ask a Saviour's
blessing upon our work. 'Ask such things
as ye need, in faith, believing, and they
shall be granted to you.' God's promises
are 'yea' and 'amen.'

"The Rector of the Parish will give us

such aid and encouragement as will greatly
benefit us, and we shall become thoroughly
awakened to the fact that we are living to
some purpose, if we but persevere. Bring
with you your young friends and companions, and let us have a large Bible Class,
such a Class as was the praise of the whole
city, when superintended in this Church
under Dr. Bedell, by Mr. Claxton; such a
Bible Class as shall reflect credit on ourselves, and redound to the .praise and
glory of God.   What a glorious work you
have before you, to bring immortal souls
into the fold of Christ, to lend your efforts
in redeeming, regenerating, and saving
your brethren !   How many blessings you
secure for yourselves !   What a great
multitude of sins will be hidden, and how
you will be made to rejoice and be glad !

" My dear young friends, will you then
help me to do good ?   Will you accept
these homely, practical remarks in kindness, and act upon their suggestions, so
that whilst we endeavor to secure for ourselves blessings innumerable, we may
faithfully labor ' to win souls to Christ.'

"God grant that we may unitedly go to work in the Lord's vineyard, where 'we shall reap, if we faint not.'

"It is my intention to open the exercise punctually at 9 o'clock, and to close precisely at 10. Please assist me, and encourage me at all times by your punctuality and regularity."

Mr. Godwin then proceeded to give a sketch of the History of the Bible, and a few extracts will well illustrate his forcible method of interesting his hearers, for he spared no trouble in seeking out instructive information.

Speaking of the length of time the Bible was in assuming its present dimensions, he says: "Dr. Allibone has been engaged for sixteen years on his great work, in two volumes, called the Dictionary of Authors; Gibbon, an Englishman, was twenty years in writing a history of 'The Decline and Fall of the Roman Empire;' Adam Clarke spent twenty-six years in writing his Commentary; Bancroft spent thirty-five years on his History; Noah Webster thirty-six years on his Dictionary. A long time, a very long time, each of these authors devoted to hard and laborious study for the benefit of mankind. The Bible was accumulating for fifteen hundred years. Yes, from the time Moses wrote Genesis, till St. John wrote the Apocalypse, all these long years had passed away."

To give an idea of the differences among the writers, Mr. Godwin said: "There were engaged in writing the Bible—Moses and Samuel, and David, and Solomon, and Ezra, and Isaiah, and all the prophets of the Old Testament; and in the New Testament, Matthew, and Mark, and Luke, and John, and Paul, and Peter, and others, over thirty persons altogether. And look, for a moment, at the difference in profession, intellect, and position, between them —Moses and Paul, men of great learning; Matthew and Peter, unlearned; David and Solomon, kings; Daniel, a prince; some were shepherds, some were farmers, some were fishermen, one was a tentmaker."

With his great love for the Bible, it would be natural to suppose that Mr. Godwin would speak in no uncertain terms about the Divine Inspiration of Holy Scripture: "God did all the thinking of the Bible! The thoughts are all God's thoughts, the wisdom all His wisdom, the mosaic workmanship of fitting every part nicely together, God's workmanship. Thirty men did the writing. God dictated the whole, and so a perfect arrangement was the result. St. Paul says: 'All Scripture is given by inspiration of God' (2 Tim. iii : 16), and what is inspiration? To inspire is, to breathe into. God breathed into their minds just what to write. St. Peter says, 'they spake as they were moved by the Holy Ghost' (2 Pet. i : 21). 'Moved,' here undoubtedly means 'told.' They said and wrote just what the Holy Ghost told them. God inspired these men to write the thirty-nine books of the Old Testament, and the twenty-seven books of the New Testament, together forming a grand harmony, and presenting a beautiful picture of Jesus and His salvation."

Mr. Godwin's love for the Word of Truth was so great that he exclaimed :— " There is no other book in the world that has been so much studied as the Bible. There is no other book that will bear to be studied as the Bible will. We tire of all other books ; but in the Bible we always find something interesting, something new, and something profitable. The books which men make are like wells, or little ponds of water ; some deeper than others, but yet we can find the bottom by seeking for it. God's book—the Bible—is like the ocean, in some places so shallow that a child can wade through it ; in others, so deep that a giant might swim in it ; the bottom is unfathomable."

The concluding words of an address,

which, judging from the results, stirred up great enthusiasm, are truly characteristic of the ardent Christian spirit of the man : " Let me now entreat you to make a right use of this Holy Book. It will do you no good to have it, unless you use it properly. Use it as the sailor does his compass. You cannot reach the haven of rest, unless the Bible is your compass. This blessed compass will always point you in the right direction. It will lead you to Jesus, your Saviour, and to your heavenly home at last. May God, indeed, grant us this for Christ's sake. Amen."

It cannot, in the light of what has been said above, be a matter for surprise that Mr. Godwin was deeply attached to this Bible Class ; that he was in his place punctually and regularly, and that he allowed nothing to interfere with this great duty. He had an assistant in the young man who was the solitary scholar on October 3d, 1869, ready to take his place in an emer-

gency; but he very rarely availed himself
of this relief. This is well exemplified in
two quotations from his journal:

OCTOBER 24th, 1869. "Having suffered
very much during the week with inflam-
matory rheumatism in the left arm, shoul-
der, and head, I was fearful that I should
be prevented from being with my Class;
but God, in His goodness, decreased the
pain, and I was punctually at my post."

MAY 15th, 1870. "A beautiful morning,
but my heart is almost crushed within me.
My darling boy Harry has had, and still
has, a severe attack of Scarlet Fever. My
wife also is very sick. God grant that the
life of my darling boy may be spared, and
my loved companion be restored to health.
With heart bowed down, I went to my
Class and delivered a lecture on 'The
Good Samaritan.' "

On MAY 22d, 1870, he wrote: "My darling boy (spared only by the direct inter-
position of Providence) is better."

The place which his Bible Class occupied
in his heart may again be gathered from

the prayer offered up by him on January 2d, 1870, when the number present had increased to twenty-five : " May God bless us yet more in increase and blessing, so that we may advance His kingdom upon earth, and do good and get good."

THE FIRST BIBLE STUDY.

———

"Thou must thyself be true,
If thou the truth wouldst teach;
Thy soul must overflow, if thou
Another's soul would reach.
It needs the overflow of heart
To give the lips full speech."

When Mr. Godwin was addressing an
audience, the strongly magnetic power of
his individuality was very striking. It is
not too much to say that he held men
within his grasp while speaking to them,
and thus enabled them to carry away lasting impressions from his teachings. The
following notes of the first " Bible Study,"
delivered to the Young Men's Bible Class
of St. Andrew's Church, will exemplify,
better than any comments the careful
method, the clear arrangement, the devout
and truth-inspiring character of his instruc-

tion ; and to these valuable principles may, under God, be traced the remarkable success with which Mr. Godwin met in every sphere of his Christian work.

"In our Introductory Lecture we spoke particularly of some of the outside features of the Bible. It is now our intention to commence a series of lessons from the inside of that good Book ; where, as I have anticipated in our Introduction, we shall find wonders of love, wonders of wisdom, wonders of power, and wonders of goodness, which, taken all together, contain heights and depths and lengths and breadths of love and wisdom 'which pass man's understanding.'

"Let us, my dear young friends, read and meditate and study the truths taught by inspired wisdom. You and I are not too learned to gather information from 'this wonderful Book.'

"In studying to profit, I would reiterate my fixed convictions and the heartfelt experience of all true Christians, that to properly understand these divine teachings, there must be a dependence on God, a reconciliation between our Master and ourselves, an earnest, devout, and believing prayer for ability to comprehend, and grace to retain, the iterated and reiterated promises vouchsafed to us in His word. If we pursue this course, and go to the fountain-head of all knowledge and goodness, the rough places will be made smooth, the difficult passages be made plain, and we shall speedily realize the truth and appreciate the information we receive. It is a certain fact, as true as God's immutable law, that for the simple asking, with faith to believe that we shall receive that which we ask, nothing will be denied us by our Heavenly Father which is consistent with His great wisdom, nothing which is best suited to our good. There are thousands who have experienced a change of heart, who have passed from the midnight darkness of sin into the marvellous light of God's countenance, who bear testimony to the fact that no good thing will be withheld from those who love God and keep His Commandments.

"Unite with me, then, in prayer to God for the outpouring of His Holy Spirit upon each of our hearts ; so that we may properly understand our lessons, and become more eminently fitted for the world's association. It is a false and self-righteous notion, that we can understand God's word and be fitted for life's cares, through self-dependence. Let me assure you, in the beginning of our Lessons, that our instruction will be all in vain, our coming together a mere farce, if we forget God, or neglect to ask in solemn, serious earnestness for His aid and guidance, as we continue from Sabbath to Sabbath to consider portions of the inside of His Holy Word.

"The Lesson chosen for to-day is taken from Luke ii : 8–20 inclusive : '*The Shepherds of Bethlehem.*'

"As shepherds were watching their flocks by night, ' all seated on the ground,' near Bethlehem (*in the same country as Bethlehem*), an Angel of the Lord appeared and glory shone around. So bright was the glory which accompanied this Angel, that the shepherds became sore afraid ;

but this fear was soon dispelled by the Angel when he said, 'Fear not, for behold I bring you good tidings of great joy which shall be to all people.' This told to them the fact of the birth of their Saviour, of our Saviour, of the Saviour of all who put their trust in Him. As soon as the Angel left them, they determined to go into Bethlehem and find out the facts for themselves. They went in great haste, and found out the truth of this revelation from God—they returned 'glorifying and praising God for all the things they had heard and seen.'

"This is a short and concise synopsis of the shepherds' connection with the verses read. We will now consider each verse, and try by frequent questions and recapitulation, to come to a good understanding of them.

"*Verse 8.* '*Same country,*' i. e., near Bethlehem. *Bethlehem* means—*the house of bread.* See Gen. xxxv: 19. 'And Rachel died: and was buried in the way to Ephrath, which is Bethlehem.' Micah v: 2. 'But thou, Bethlehem Ephratah,' etc. 'Bethlehem Ephratah'—*fruitful house of bread.* This may suggest to us that Jesus, who was born here, is the ' Bread of Life.' (John vi : 48). 'I am that bread of life.'

" Bethlehem is six miles S W. of Jerusalem—so small as not to be named among the cities of Judah. David was born here, hence it is called 'the City of David' (v. 11). Only 3000 inhabitants. A convent now stands over the supposed place of Nativity, and a silver star is placed over what is shown as the exact spot. Rachel's tomb is two miles out of Bethlehem. (Gen. xlviii : 7.)

" '*Keeping watch.'* Compare David (1 Sam. xvii : 34) in his time watching against wild beasts ; in the time of Jesus, shepherds watched against robbers. Shepherds had need of vigilance, patience, tenderness, and courage—Jesus is the Good Shepherd. Compare John x : 14 ; Heb. xiii : 20 ; Psalm xxiii ; Psalm xcv : 7 ; Psalm cxxi : 3.

" *Verse* 9. '*Angel'* signifies—messenger ; *evangel* means a good message, usually applied to the Gospel ; *evangelist*—a Gospel messenger.

" '*Came upon,'* descended, appeared.

"'*Glory of the Lord,*' etc.   Compare the '*Shechinah*' (Exodus xxiv: 16; Numbers xiv: 10).   Angels were much interested in the life and work of Jesus (Matt. iv: 11; xxviii: 2–7).   (Luke xxii: 43.)

"'*Sore afraid,*' the vision was so unexpected and glorious.

"*Verse* 10 '*Good tidings*' signifies good news.   Gospel, good news from God.   *To all people*, so far did the old promise reach (Gen. xxii: 18); (Matt. xxviii: 19); (Luke xxiv: 47).

"*Verse* 11. '*Saviour,*' *Jesus* means *Saviour* (Matt. i: 21).   *Christ* means *anointed*. *Christ Jesus*, the Anointed Saviour.   *Joshua*, Hebrew for Jesus; *Messiah*, Hebrew for Christ (John i: 41, margin).

"*Verse* 12. '*Sign.*'   The sign consisted not in His being a *babe*, nor in *swaddling clothes;* but that He was *lying in a manger*, a stable, a place for cattle ; perhaps it was a cave.   Probably there were other babes, but only one in such a place.

"'*No room.*'   He was thus early 'cast out and rejected.'

"'*Inn.*' Probably one of the large caravanserai, or khans, provided for the use of pilgrims. Very few inns now-a-days find room for Jesus.

"*Verse* 13. '*Suddenly*,' etc. A multitude of angels came to confirm the message of one, to express their own joy, and remove any doubt from the shepherds' minds. Angels sang for joy when the Saviour was born, and they sing now for joy, when a saved soul is born, for we must be 'born again' (Luke xv : 7–10).

"*Verse* 14. The angels' word stated the end of the Saviour's coming—to the highest *glory* of God, *peace* between God and man, and man and man, and also *good will* (John iii : 16, 17); (2 Cor. v : 19).

"*Verse* 15. '*The shepherds said*,' they were too astonished before to speak. Now they doubted not the vision ; hence they were prompt in obeying.

"*Verse* 16. '*They came with haste.*' They were joyous and eager. Had they delayed they would have missed the sight. By seeing the sign they proved the truth of the message.

"*Verse* 17. '*They made known abroad.*'

Sight gave them boldness—they were bold
to speak. He who hath both seen and
heard will be bolder than he who has only
heard.

"*Verse* 18. '*Wondered.*' Well they
might! How should these shepherds have
known if they had not been told?

"*Verse* 19. '*But Mary*,' etc. Here was
another sign for her. She, doubtless, wondered also. How the recollection of this
must have comforted her heart in after
years!

"*Verse* 20. '*Praising God*,' not thinking
so much of the angels, or their own de-
serts, as of the goodness of Him who had
at last visited His people. To Him our
grateful thanks should rise.

"From the foregoing we draw as a reasonable and, I trust, a profitable conclusion,
the following analysis:

"I. *The Preacher.* 'An Angel' never
undertook a more gladsome task, or more
gladly did the Master's will. Angels have
often been executioners of wrath; they are
now the messengers of mercy. None need
be ashamed of Jesus, since even a multi-

tude of angels delighted to confess Him.
Let us all, every member of the Class,
preach Jesus. Even a child may preach
Christ, and turn some to repentance.
Each and every one of us (if we but try)
may become preachers of Jesus. An
Angel was the first preacher of the Gospel. The 'glad tidings' of the last day
will be proclaimed by an Angel. (1 Thess.
iv : 16). 'For the Lord Himself shall descend from heaven with a shout, with voice
of the archangel, and with the trump of
God : and the dead in Christ shall rise first.'

"The Angel, a pattern preacher, short
and to the point.

"The glory of Christ, and of the Gospel, may be inferred from the nature and
character of the preacher. Not even great
kings had such a herald as Jesus, who was
greater than Solomon, had.

"II. *The Congregation.* Shepherds, rep-
resentative men, The good tidings were
not given to princes, who are few, but to
peasants, who are many. The Gospel is
for all (Matt. xi : 5 ; Mark xii : 37). 'The
poor have the Gospel preached to them,'

and ' the common people heard him gladly.'
They are poor, indeed, without religion,
rich with it. The poor need more than
any 'good news and glad tidings.' These
poor shepherds were thought of. They
were at their proper work, when the angel
came. See, in many instances, illustrations
of God meeting men when at their duties
—David was keeping his sheep when the
message came from Samuel, etc. It was
night when they heard the angel. This
was light in darkness. Bright light in the
night of sorrow, the night of poverty, of
ignorance, etc. (Job xxxvii: 21). 'And
now men see not the bright light which is
in the clouds : but the wind passeth, and
cleanseth them.'

"III. *The Sermon.* The keynote of all
religious teaching since—very short, only
a few sentences, easily remembered, very
pointed. The angel went at once to the
root of the matter—very comprehensive,
he preached ' peace' and ' good will'—very
demonstrable, there was a sign following—
very powerful, the shepherds, who feared
at first, were made joyful and bold. The

'good news' turns our fear into joy, if we believe the tidings.

"Now, my dear young friends, we may greatly profit by these verses, and learn :

" 1. That those who publish Jesus rank with the angels.

" 2. That however poor and unworthy, however ignorant and despised we may be, the Gospel is sent to each one of us individually.

" 3. That God usually blesses men if engaged in their lawful, proper work ; such work is praiseworthy and honorable.

"4. That the Gospel of our Lord and Saviour Jesus Christ produces both gladness and boldness.

" 5. That those who receive the Gospel should do their utmost to make it known.

" 6. That even poor shepherds may enter into the joy and labor of the holy and mighty angels.

"We will reserve the glory of the Nativity of our Blessed Saviour for some future lesson ; but to take up these points :

"1. A sweet, little darling, scarcely in her teens, said to her mother : ' I want to do something for Jesus. Hand me the Bible, that I may learn something from its inspired pages, something to do for my precious Saviour.' That girl found those dear, consoling words, which were as 'a sweet morsel under her tongue'—'But if any man love God, the same is known of Him.'

" 'I will go and tell my friends and schoolmates that if they love God, He knows it, and He will make them happy, and, oh, what happiness to be known of God!' She ran to do her first work for the Master, to 'preach' the Gospel and publish Jesus. She lived to see many converted through her instrumentality, held rank with the angels on earth, and has now become an angel in heaven. That dear loved one was my own sister.

"It is not only the man called of God and set apart by ecclesiastical appointment, who is to publish 'the glad tidings,' but you and I also—the shepherd, the merchant, the lawyer, the physician, the little girl, the school-boy, the young and old, the rich

and the poor—all can publish Christ and
rank with the angels.

"At one of our Union Prayer Meetings,
I heard a Missionary from the far West
say that whilst God had blessed his efforts
in pointing two souls to the Great Shepherd of their salvation in his field of labor
during the past year, a single layman had
influenced twenty to join the church. That
man published Jesus and ranks with the
Angels. What a good and glorious work
to publish Jesus and rank with the Angels
who told the news of His birth to the humble shepherds !

"2. It is a soul-inspiring thought that the
blessed Gospel is given to each of us individually. Whatever our condition in life,
whether as shepherds, or as millionaires,
the truths of the Gospel belong to us, and
are sent to us by God himself for our
edification, instruction and benefit. I have
seen the poverty-stricken, care-worn mendi-
cant receive and enjoy the blessings of the
Gospel upon the street, as much as we are
doing now, in this comfortable room, clothed
in our good apparel and rich in creature

comforts. Thank God that the Gospel is sent to all, and is free to all. Do we properly appeciate this fact, my dear young friends, and will we to-day decide to show our appreciation by resolving on good works for the future? God grant it.

"3. There is no doubt in my mind that God always blesses those who receive and publish the Gospel. It may be in the providence of God that trouble comes upon the just, as well as upon the unjust; but whilst affliction of body, or mind, or both, may visit the righteous, yet they will never be forsaken, nor their seed beg bread. The righteous will eventually prosper in the work of their hands. Every day's observation convinces both you and me, that, although it may be slow, yet the yield of fruit to the faithful husbandman is sure; whilst those who are engaged in wicked traffic, although flourishing for a time like a green bay tree, are at last cut down and followed by blight and mildew all through life's journey.

"4. Go with me into that miserable hovel, the abode of slavery and poverty.

See that colored man without the knowledge of a single letter of the alphabet.
He is praying with all his soul to his Master
in Heaven. Hear the inspired language
and the beautiful quotations from Holy
Writ. This is the boldness and gladness
produced by the Gospel of our Lord Jesus
Christ.

"Look at that modest, blushing, young
lady. She begins to talk of Christ to her
companion in the crowded room. See how
her eyes sparkle, hear her eloquent and
persuasive language. This is the boldness
and gladness of the Gospel.

"Behold that young man just from the
Divinity School. Tremblingly he ascends
the pulpit. He turns to the Word of God.
He reads about Jesus. He begins to talk
about Jesus. He becomes firm, zealous,
determined. This is the boldness and
gladness of the Gospel.

"5. Are we true to ourselves; are we
true to our Maker if we receive the Gospel and hide our light under a bushel; if
we enjoy the great blessings of the knowledge of godliness and yet quietly pass our

days without spreading broadcast its comfort of peace and good-will; if we say to our souls ' take thine ease,' whilst hundreds of thousands are perishing for the very knowledge we possess? No! my dear young friends, let us rather be up and doing—doing our utmost to impart our knowledge of the Gospel, and thus contribute towards the salvation of those around us. If we have but one talent let us use that one ; if five, let us use the five for the glory of God.

" 6. Did you and I ever think that it is our privilege to enter into the joy and labor of the holy and mighty Angels. Indeed we can participate with them in saving souls through Christ. We can be co-workers with them in spreading the Gospel far and wide.

" I pray you then join with me henceforward in the joy and labor of working for Christ, and God will abundantly bless both you and me, and, best of all, will save us with an everlasting salvation."

LITERARY EXTRACTS.

———

" Speak to me low, my Saviour, low and sweet
From out the hallelujahs, sweet and low,
Lest I should fear and fall, and miss Thee so,
Who art not missed by any that entreat."

BROWNING.

About the time that Mr. Godwin left the Sunday School connected with St. Andrew's Church and took charge of the Bible Class, he published a small, but very suggestive book, entitled " A Companion for the Sunday School Teacher." The bent of his mind is well seen in some favorite quotations which he inserts at the beginning of the work :

" Wisdom is oftentimes nearer when we stoop than when we soar."

" He prayeth best who loveth best
All things both great and small ;
For the dear God who loveth us,
He made and loveth all."

"Let us not be weary in well doing, for in due season we shall reap, if we faint not."

Another most expressive one may be added :

" ' Jesus only !' Let us sum up all that we have learned of spiritual truth in these two blessed words. Jesus Christ's commandments—our law ; His perfect example —our guide ; His intercession—our hope ; His death—our life ; His love—our portion forever."

The book, unpretentious though it is, doubtless gives us the results of Mr. Godwin's own experience which, as has been recorded, was by no means insignificant.

"To be successful," he says, "in our labors in the Sabbath School, so expressively termed ' the nursery of the Christian Church,' punctuality and regularity in attendance are among the first of the many requisites ; and the divine blessing that always rests upon those who supplicate it, should earnestly be asked upon the duties of the day."

These were among the principles which he carried out in his daily life—strict punctuality, regularity and prayerfulness.

In one especial passage we seem to be beholding, as in a picture, the very life of the man:—"Though the faith of the teacher may at times pass through the severest trials, we should never omit the performance of our *entire* duty 'in the patience of hope and the labor of love,' leaving the result in the hands of Him whom we serve, and who will never fail to bless and sanctify the effort of the teacher who, in sincerity and singleness of purpose, seeks to win souls to Christ, and lives, in his own walk and conversation, the life whose joys he seeks to share with those committed to his charge."

How truly these words describe the spirit which actuated him, not only as a teacher in the Sunday School and the Bible

Class, but as the head of the family of men whom he gathered round him in later years. Ever a careful student of the Word of God, it will be of interest to glance at the warm-hearted way in which he recommends the study of it:

" I hold it as a cardinal point in the duty of the Sabbath-school teacher, to be an industrious and prayerful reader of the sacred Scriptures. To impart soul-saving truths to the lambs of God's flock, unless we have first gathered them from that sublime and inspired volume, is not possible. Without this preparation, our teaching will be in vain. If we rely upon our own weak and defective knowledge, and trust to our own powers we shall fail in the mission we have undertaken. There are treasures enough in that volume—there is sufficient brightness in that single spark of celestial light —to illumine a thousand worlds. There is in it sufficient material for study to occupy us to the end of time.

" Gems of purest lustre sparkle upon its pages, treasures of inestimable value are found in its inexhaustible store-houses, riches of wisdom beyond all the lore of sages, wisdom from on high—descend in all the plentitude of a divine bounty upon the readers of its precious promises ; a river of the water of life flows from the springs of its truth, to which who thirst may 'come and take freely' That river, always running, is never dry. Read and re-read it, again and again, and you have new springs of the purest waters, sweet dews descend upon your soul, new mines of choicest diamonds, new sources of light and knowledge unknown, unfound in any other book ; what better instructor, what more reliable guide can we have than the sublime and elevating truths iterated and re-iterated from Genesis to the Apocalypse? How full of lasting, loving, soul-cheering truths to the faithful ! How fraught with warning to the evil-doer ! How much joy, and consolation for those who do aright ! How admonitory and threatening to the sinner ! We ourselves can learn and im-part to our classes from this inspired work all that is useful, beneficial and interesting.

Why then ever seek for instruction of doubtful bearing? Remember this great blessing, He has given us a reliable and divine book of instruction, we would substitute nothing in its place. We would study its pages upon our knees, asking God to give us divine wisdom that we may be useful workers in his vineyards and learn from His prophet Daniel ' that they that be wise shall shine as the brightness of the firmament.' "

Mr. Godwin goes on to describe the ultimate purpose of the teacher, thus :

" Our one great aim as teachers should be to incline the mind of the scholar to look upward toward the source of all happiness—' The Great Head of the Church ;' to view all things else as insignificant compared with the unspeakable love of God ; to impress thoroughly upon the young and tender heart the beauties of godliness— that through Christ we can do all things, that without him we can do nothing ; that, while secular instruction is proper and necessary in all, that pertains to this life, yet the world's knowledge must become subservient to a knowledge of godliness or it profiteth nothing ; that God is Love, and that we should love Him, as He loves us."

It is well-known that Mr. Godwin never looked back when, to use his favorite expression, "he had put his hand to the plough ;" although there were times when he declared that he felt inclined "to lie down by the wayside." The spirit which supported him may be gathered from the cheering words he pens for his fellow-laborers :

"We should never be disheartened or downcast by what seems to be failure in our efforts. We must not be too hasty in expecting germination in the seed that we have sown. Our Lord, in His parable of the Sower, has taught us His lesson in this respect. Our beloved Redeemer, who died that all might be saved, had but few true followers, and did His Father's work under discouragement of which we can have but faint conception. In His extremest

agony some of those whom He had most
favored slept while He suffered, and all afterwards forsook Him and fled. He was
fulfilling His Master's mission ; He was
engaged in the work which He completed
only when He uttered His expiring groan
upon the accursed tree. If those for whom
we labor and pray are regardless of our
solicitude, and give no heed to our teachings and example, let us rather redouble
than relax our zeal, lest remissness be
charged to the account that we must render
at the Great Day. Paul never ceased to
plant, nor Apollos to water, realizing that
God alone could give the increase."

And again :—'' Be not discouraged then,
dear teacher, for ' no effort is lost,' if sanctified by God. ' The ways of wisdom are
pleasantness and all her paths are peace.'
Remember with heart-cheering consolation,
that we are co-workers with the Almighty
in hastening the universal reign of the
Prince of Peace, in promoting the good of
those under our charge ; we are advancing
the kingdom of Christ, and with the blessing of God our success will be proportionate

to the excellence of the objects we have in view. God's promises are yea and amen."

How faithfully he practised what he laid down in his precepts, the world will never know, for only those who came personally, day by day, into contact with it, can realize the consistency of his character.

Those who have been connected with him in the great work of his life, during the last seventeen years, know full well what rough material frequently came under his hand. Again in this little manual for the teacher—this mirror of his mind, as it were —we find a key to his success :

" There are moments in the life of every teacher when irresolution and discouragement attend upon baffled efforts and unpromising toil. Inattention, waywardness, disrespect on the part of the scholar, often chill our ardor, and temporarily disqualify us for the work we have undertaken ; but with the sober second thought, these trifling annoyances, which can be eventually corrected, weigh but lightly in that balance which on the other side is heavy with the rich and lasting results of faithful labor. These seeming troubles are but 'trifles light as air' in comparison with the great and lasting benefits bestowed—benefits greater by far than gold or rubies, for the one perisheth, the other is everlasting. The most disobedient and unruly boy of a Sunday School class of twelve, in 1850, is now one of the most eminent and successful divines. This is no unusual fact—no isolated case. It teaches us that by patient and continuous effort, with God's blessing, the least promising seed, with faithful culture, may eventually bear abundant and eternal fruit. The uncouth, unseemly exterior may contain a good true heart within. Under the most trying circumstance therefore we should not be discouraged. We are working in the vineyard of the Lord; there may be spots of unproductive soil, but let each of us strive, with earnest prayer and unvarying patience, to improve that portion of it that God has intrusted to our care. He will reward our efforts."

One may well ask—what was the *motive* of such a life as that of Mr. Godwin ? The spring of action is not far to seek, and is again best given in his own words :

" With *love to Christ* as the great motive power which impels us to labor faithfully in our calling, and the *love of Christ* as our consolation, we can accomplish astonishing results. Our hearts by the indwelling of the Holy Spirit being full of life, light, joy, we shall ever be ready to realize every conviction of duty and act decidedly and successfully. Influenced by our love to Christ we view those around us as our brethren and are disposed ' to work while it is called day,' to assume and perform the duties of our calling with joy and gladness; with the knowledge that we work for our Saviour in view, our thoughts are inspired, our wisdom increased, and there is power and efficacy in our teaching."

It was also in such visions as the following that Samuel P. Godwin regarded the end of his labors :

" The saving of one immortal soul repays the most arduous labor of a life time. The bread cast upon the waters will be gathered after many days ; the seed sown in weakness will ultimately become a fruitful tree.   God will reward our efforts whatever the discouragement by the wayside. With prayer, pains, patience, and perseverance, there will be a golden harvest to garner by and by, and God's blessing, even His own blessing, will be our sweetest reward."

In 1867 Mr. Godwin published " Heart-Breathings "—a small volume of meditations and Prayers.

One only of these can here be given, but it is sufficiently indicative of the depth to which that great heart could be stirred.

" ' I waited patiently for the Lord, and He inclined unto me and heard my calling.'

"We approach the fountain of all happiness this morning, realizing our own unworthiness, conscious of our short comings, and fully aware that we can offer no plea, through any merit of our own, in extenuation of our own sinfulness ; poor, weak, miserable sinners, we do not deserve the slightest recognition from Thee; yet O, precious Saviour, we can rely on Thy promises, and through Thy intercession be made to rejoice that we have been with Christ and learned of Him. We thank Thee, good Lord, for the simpleness of prayer, for the efficacy of prayer, for that divine joy and comfort imparted through prayer, but above all that we are thus privileged to converse with Thee, our adorable Redeemer and receive that wisdom and comfort of which the world knows nothing. Give us faith continually to believe in Thy precious promises, that we may the more abundantly realize Thy goodness towards us, and evidence to others the truthfulness of our profession, that they 'seeing our good works, may glorify our Father who is in Heaven.' We would implore Thy presence with us, that we may be instant in season and out of season, in glorifying Thy holy name, thereby influencing those around us to good works. We would ask Thy special blessing, glorified Redeemer, upon our beloved family ; save them from evil, shield them from harm ; protect them under the shadow of Thy wings, that we may be a 'household of faith and a family of prayer ;' give us the ability to bring up our children in the ' fear and admonition of the Lord ;' by precept and example ; may they learn of us as we learn of Christ, so that with us they may live and die, an honor and a blessing to all ; prepare the hearts of our darlings that they may right early seek the Lord and find Him to the joy and comfort of their souls. Bless those who are in any manner connected with us by the ties of nature. Grant to those who profess Thy name the divine unction from on high, that they may attain more abundantly to the holiness of the Lord ; that they may be saved from the devices of the evil one ; that they may be comforted in all the sorrows of life. Constrain the hearts of those who know Thee not, ' to turn to the Lord and seek salvation ;' may they see the sinfulness of sin ; may they be convinced that the world's pleasures are fleeting and visionary, that in God's favor only can true joys be found ; turn their hearts, turn their hearts,

O Lord, towards Thy cross, that they may apply for and receive Thy blessings; especially do our petitions ascend for those, who regarding not Thy commandments would find happiness outside Thy fold; convict, convert, sanctify and save them, we implore Thee.

" Bless all for whom it is our duty to pray—the sick and the suffering, the poor and the needy, the fatherless and widow, the distressed and disconsolate, wherever they may be—and hasten on the glorious time when all the nations of the earth shall rejoice as we rejoice, and the desert shall bloom and blossom as the rose. Go with us into the world and its cares; protect us from evil thoughts; make us just and upright in all our dealings; and grant that we enter not into temptation. Hear our prayers, O Lord; answer our petitions, and we will ascribe all the glory to Thee our most blessed Saviour, for ever. Amen."

In these days there is a strong tendency to suppose that when men, with the strong religious principles which characterized Mr.

Godwin, come to deal with the practical
questions of the business and social world
they are impracticable and eccentric. There
could not be a greater mistake as far as
Mr. Godwin was concerned. He would
teach us that, if we forget to-day's social life
and duty in the preparation for that future
of happiness, we are as much in error as if
we forget the future in the ever present
to-day.

A lecture delivered by him at the Young
Men's Christian Association for Colored
People, is sufficient to show the remarkable
degree in which his mind was alive to the
necessity of a proper training for the business of daily life.   He said :

" Brethren, what is the *Duty* of the *Hour ?*
What is your present *duty*, especially in
consideration of the high and holy blessings
which God has conferred upon you and
your race ?

" Bear in mind, my brethren, ' He who
is false in the present duty, breaks a thread

in the loom, and will find the flaw when he has forgotten the cause.' Look around you, go on the watchtower of self-examination, ask God to direct your footsteps, and your present duty will become as plain to you as your present existence.

"First, then, it is an imperative duty to sow the seeds of a thorough, practical and scientific education in your own households and among your brethren.

"There is a social status that can never be reached in ignorance. *As the revealed light of Christianity increases and assumes its just proportions, secular education will be the more required to meet its demands.* Impress the necessity of education upon those of riper years, and make it obligatory upon those who are young. We say it in all Christian love and boldness, my brethren, that it is your present duty to become educated up to your privileges. It is as necessary for social and political equality that your minds should be educated to their capacities, as it is for your bodies to be fed in order to be strengthened for their daily labor. Polite society demands intelligence, and God will hold you accountable, if you neglect your duty, and refuse to acquire it. But, say you, how are we to fulfil this duty? Avail yourselves of the many opportunities presented to you ; send your children to the public schools ; teach yourselves by earnest application, and then teach your less favored brethren."

Mr. Godwin thus described some of the advantages of a good education, showing that while ever regardful of everlasting interests he was not forgetful of temporal blessings :

"We view the duty of being educated as one of the most essential duties of the hour. With a cultivated intellect and with religion in the heart, that which otherwise can be accomplished only in ages, may be done in years ; social, political and religious privileges may be secured ; your own good subserved, and the intention of God toward you be fully realized. It is an incontrovertible fact, that ignorance debases humanity, while it is equally true that intelligence exalts it ; however humble or deformed that man may be who has a cultivated mind, he rises in dignity in the estimation of his fellow-men, as his intellectual attainments shine out from his mind, and illuminate the sphere in which he moves."

Whenever Mr. Godwin spoke, the remarkable richness and appositeness of his illustrations struck all his hearers, and those who knew him most intimately can recognize the undercurrent which prompted him in the selection. In the lecture from which the above quotations are taken there is an illustration which has a peculiar interest, as describing the whole aim and object of Mr. Godwin's life :

"The Rev. John Newton said : 'I see in this world two heaps ; the one of human happiness, the other of misery. Now, if I can take but the smallest bit from one and add to the other, I carry a point. If as I go home, a child dropped a halfpenny, and if by giving it another, I can wipe away its tears, I feel that I have done something ; I should be glad indeed to do greater things ; but I will not neglect this.' "

But Mr. Godwin can never be thoroughly understood until his prayerful habits are appreciated. It was by prayer that he lived and worked. His meditations in "Heart-Breathings" are evidence of this, but perhaps he allowed the outside world a brighter glance of the recesses of his heart, when on that platform of this Colored Young Men's Christian Association he spoke these remarkable words:

"Brethren, it is in the mount of prayer that God is seen; even when the Christian goes up the hill towards duty with a heavy heart, because, as yet, he can have no sight of Him. Turn not therefore back, but go on with courage, He may be nearer than you think. 'In that same hour,' said Christ, 'it shall be given unto you.'

"Abraham's servant prays, Rebekah appears; Jacob wrestles in prayer, and prevails with Christ; Moses prays, Amalek is discomfited; Joshua prays, Achan is discovered; Hannah prays, Samuel is born; Elisha prays, Jordan is divided; Asa prays,

a victory is gained; Jehosaphat cries unto
God, and his foes are turned away; Isaiah
and Hezekiah pray, 185,000 Assyrians are
dead in twelve hours; Daniel prays, the
lions' mouths are stopped; Mordecai and
Esther fast, Haman is hanged on his own
gallows in three days; Ezra prays at Ahara,
God answers; Nehemiah utters a prayer,
the king's heart is softened in a moment.
Prayer reaches to eternity."

"In the silence of your closet, seek God
in secret prayer; in your places of business
look up to Him in fervent supplication;
around the family fireside offer up your
sincere petitions; in the sanctuary let your
thoughts ascend above the groveling earth
and hold communion with God. At all
times, and in all places, let your requests
be made known to the Author and Giver
of every good and perfect gift, for knowledge to conceive, wisdom to arrange, and
strength to perform your duty, and you
will receive that spiritual wisdom and
ghostly strength which will prepare you to
meet the responsibilities of the hour. In
your own strength, you may accomplish

something, but in the strength of God, great and wonderful things, whereof your hearts will be made glad, and your fellow-citizens and brethren will come fully up to that standard of excellence wherein their just proportions will be developed."

THE THEORY OF DRUNKENNESS.

———

" Nihil aliud est ebrietas quam voluntaria insania."
SENECA.
Drunkenness is nothing but voluntary madness.

Another special phase of Mr. Godwin's character and work must now be dealt with, as being the main object of this memoir. With a heart ever open to the sufferings of humanity, of whatever kind they were, he was most deeply moved by the sin and sorrow wrought, not only on society, but on individuals, by the vice of drinking. To alleviate the misery resulting from this, to prevent it, as far as possible, from continuing to afflict the drunkard, his family and mankind around him, to assist in driving the demon out of the world and restoring the victims to a life of sobriety and steadfast fulfilment of duty, became the self-im-

posed task of his later manhood. In fact
it may be said that he felt himself called to
this work, and he spared neither himself,
nor his substance, in carrying it out as an
offering to his Heavenly Master.

As a member of the American Temperance Union, of the Sons of Temperance and
of the Order of Good Templars, as well as
of several minor kindred societies, he was
ever ready to spend and be spent in spreading those principles of Total Abstinence
which are the characteristic features of such
organizations.

He was a forcible and eloquent advocate.
It mattered not where, or when, a need
arose ; he occupied the platform of the
Total Abstinence cause on every possible
occasion, traveling at his own expense, and
receiving no reward but gratitude for his
services.   Not only in his own city of Philadelphia ; not only in the State of Pennsylvania, even in the remote parts ; but in
every neighboring State, his voice was

heard, advocating those principles which he felt were the only safeguards against the vicious habit of intemperance.

No movement in the Temperance cause ever found him unsympathetic, no Temperance mission had to ask in vain for his support. But unlike many of the valuable and energetic body of Temperance Reformers, Mr. Godwin was not a mere theorist; he was above all things a practical man. He was not content to address a multitude, to impress and excite susceptible hearts, and then to call up the conscience stricken and the terror stricken to the table, to administer a pledge of total abstinence and to send forth the neophyte, bound by a solemn vow, into the very same surroundings, the very same associates, the very same opportunities for sin which lay in the path in which he had been walking. His method was a practical one. It was this— to separate the victim of drunkenness, for awhile, from all his former surroundings ;

then, by medical treatment when necessary, by rest, quiet and habits of regularity, and by nourishing food to bring the physical powers and mental powers to a normal condition ; and when this was accomplished, nay even during its progress, to rouse a sense of sin against God and self, of weakness and inability to rise unaided. Then the pledge was to be administered and the man sent forth to his duty in the world, clad in the Christian armor. Nay, he would not leave him then. He would associate him with a brotherhood, each member of which, having gone through similar trials, would extend the hand of sympathy and afford friendship and support.

This was a new light on the field of Temperance work, and undeterred by the many and apparently insurmountable difficulties, Mr. Godwin set himself to carry into practice the course which his earnest mind had marked out. To him belongs the honor of devising and executing the one organization of the whole world which has attained the greatest success in the reformation of the inebriate.

Surely it is not inappropriate that in the " city of brotherly love " should such a scheme have been organized, and surely, also, it is not too much to say that while that city bears its name, the monuments of Mr. Godwin's work will never be allowed to fall. Those monuments are: The Franklin Reformatory Home for Inebriates of the city of Philadelphia and the Godwin Association of that " Home."

The method proposed by Mr. Godwin was not the sudden growth of an hour. It must have been developed from years of careful study of the question and an intimate knowledge of all the steps through which reformatory measures had advanced, since the time when the Temperance Standard was first raised.

With every desire, doubtless, on the part of philanthropists, to benefit the fallen,

8

for many years the nature of intemperance was misunderstood. Medical men who turned their attention to the study of the vice with a sincere desire to discover a remedy, almost to a man, concluded that habitual drunkenness is a disease; and for that disease they invented the name which has so long stood in the way of the true methods of dealing with the evil—*dipso-mania*. So late as 1871, Dr. Boddington, before the Medical Association, said:

"The confusion between drunkenness as a disease, and drunkenness as a vice, must be cleared up. For my part I look upon all habitual drunkenness as a disease, and I boldly call it all *dipsomania*. It is in its character as a disease that we as physicians are entitled to deal with it. I would sink the notion of its being a mere vicious propensity. When fully developed there are not two kinds of habitual drunkenness. The cases are, one and all, cases of dipso-mania, of irresistible, uncontrollable, morbid impulse to drink stimulants."

This statement, chosen out of very many similar ones made by able men who have made a study of drunkenness and its effects, well represents the current popular idea. From this idea, doubtless, arose the system of the isolation of inebriates for special treatment, and the subject became much more capable of investigation.

Old theories and prejudices, however, die hard, and the popular theory of drunkenness still numbers a large body of firm supporters. The Commissioners of Lunacy for Scotland, who visited the voluntary homes or asylums for inebriates in that country in 1872, '73 and '74, say:

"It is possible that prolonged compulsory abstinence from alcoholic liquors may restore to habitual drunkards the power of self-control and enable them to resist the craving to which, when at liberty, they succumb. Our experience, however, does not give us much reason to expect this result."

Nay, in 1872 their testimony goes so far as to state:

"Indeed it would not be easy to point out one single case of permanent and satisfactory reform."

The British Parliamentary Report on Habitual Drunkards, in 1872, declares as the result of all the inquiries made that:

"Occasional drunkenness may and very frequently does become confirmed and habitual and soon passes into the condition of a disease, uncontrolable by the individual, unless some extraneous influence either punitive or curative is brought into play."

These extraneous influences in this country have been exercised in the various kinds of Reformatories for Inebriates. These are of four classes:

THE HOME, into which all must enter voluntarily and honorably, expressing an earnest desire for Reformation.

THE ASYLUM, which receives a few of the above class of persons, but in which the great majority of inmates are sent

under the persuasion of friends, with little,
if any, desire for reformation, but to be
cured of a "*disease.*" The greater number
of Institutions in this country are of this
type.

THE HOUSE OF CORRECTION, where the
treatment is purely punitive, the inmates
being shut up by magistrates for various
periods as prisoners. A very small proportion of these reform, not caring for
reformation.

The fourth class is instanced in the
King's County Asylum, which is a combination of all the three above mentioned.
Here are found *the anxious, the persuaded*
and *the committed*, those having the means
being able to live luxuriously.

With regard to the treatment pursued
in the third and fourth classes, Dr. Conrad
of Maryland has said: "I do not know of
a single case where a cure has been effected
by confinement."

Reformation is mainly to be sought

among inmates of the first two classes of Institutions ; but here the disease theory holds its ground with strong persistence.

At the first meeting of the American Association for the cure of Inebriates, it was declared as an essential principle that "Intemperance is a disease."

Dr. R. P. Harris, for many years the Physician of the Franklin Home, had the temerity to state at the Fifth Annual meeting of the Association that " He regarded drunkenness as a habit, sin, or crime, and did not speak of cases being *cured*, as in a hospital, but *reformed.*" The report in which this bold assertion was made was denounced and returned to its author, with a request that it be modified in order to bring it more into accord with the declaration of the Association as given above.

Dr. R. P. Harris had, at the time he expressed this opinion, been treating some hundreds of inebriates in the Franklin Home, concerning which it cannot be out of place to quote the words of an eminent English authority, Dr. J. C. Bucknill of London. He says in an article in the February number of the Contemporary Review, of 1877 :

"My own impressions of the Inebriate Asylums of America—and I visited six of them—are most unfavorable. I believe the treatment of habitual drunkards for the cure of their supposed disease to be unsound from top to bottom and everywhere. I make no exception ; for the only institution in which I did find good, honest, earnest work being done was in the Inebriate Reformatory (the Franklin Home) at Philadelphia, in the management of which the idea of curing a disease is steadfastly put on one side. All honor is due to the devoted men and women who labor in this place at the regeneration of their fallen fellow-citizens."

Any candid person will decide which of the two theories gives the true key to reformation. By the disease theory of the sci-

entists, the victim of intemperance is taught
that reformation is practically beyond his
power, for he is suffering from an "irresistible, uncontrolable, morbid impulse."
By the second he is told that he has been
giving way to a sinful habit, from which, by
the grace of God, he may rise to newness
of life.   To this grace of God the method
inaugurated, developed, completed by the
wisdom, energy and self-devotion of Mr.
Godwin, would lead the man.

It must not be supposed for one moment that Mr. Godwin concealed from any
victim the enormity of his sin.   Here are
two of his utterances :

"Of all vices take heed of drunkenness.
Other vices are but fruits of disordered affections ; this disorders, nay, banishes reason.   Other vices impair the soul ; this
demolishes her two chief faculties, the understanding and the will.   Other vices
make their own way, this makes way for
all vices.   He that is a drunkard is qualified for all vice."

And :—" All excess is ill, but drunkenness is of the worst sort. It destroys health,
dismounts the mind, and unmans men. It
reveals secrets, is quarrelsome, lascivious,
impudent, dangerous, mad. He that is
drunk is not a man, because he is for so
long devoid of reason that distinguishes a
man from a beast."

But having brought the man to see the
depth of his sin according to the standard
that :

> " The wrong is made and measured by
>   The right's inverted dignity,"

his gentleness and tenderness were unspeakable.

> " Wouldst thou with deep repentance bring
>   A wanderer to the fold of God :
> Use not reproach—a bitter sting,
>   Or hold to view an iron rod.
> With pleasant words and looks that speak
>   The warm outgushings of the heart
> Go—the adamant will break
>   And tears of true contrition start."

His own faith in the all-powerful grace
which should raise the fallen is well brought
out in another of his " Moral Gems :"

" It appears to me that the grace of God mends the head while it governs the heart. It brings the mind into such a holy, regular frame, that we can know nothing of the good of our own existence until we exist in God."

It now becomes necessary to speak of the Foundation of the Franklin Home, the brotherhood of the Godwin Association and the methods by which Mr. Godwin's system of reformation and restoration were carried out.

THE FRANKLIN REFORMATORY HOME.

"The atmosphere
Breathes rest and comfort, and the many chambers
Seem full of welcomes."
LONGFELLOW.

On February 25th, 1872, a meeting of Delegates from the various Temperance Organizations was held in Philadelphia at 607, Walnut street, for the purpose of considering and developing some plan for improving the condition of inebriates and helping them to reform.

In the course of discussion there was urged upon the delegates the necessity of a home where the inebriate could be fed and cared for, until he was in a condition to go forth and seek his own support.

In accordance with this idea, a Committee of fifteen was appointed to report on a plan for establishing a Reformatory Home and Temporary Asylum for Inebriates. This Committee, having but a faint outline of the plan to be followed in working such an establishment, sought information in every possible quarter. In answer to inquiries, reports flowed in upon them ; but the key to the difficulty was supplied by Dr. Day, of Greenwood, Mass., who said : " Hire a house in some convenient neighborhood ; place it in the charge of one who has the heart and soul for the work and trust to Providence, time and experience for the rest."

On March 12th the Committee proposed to rent No. 911 Locust street, at an annual rental of seven hundred dollars, for the purpose indicated, and at another meeting, held on March 29th, it was reported that this had been carried out.

Mr. Samuel P. Godwin was elected the President of the "Home," and a full Board of Managers was named. To obviate a financial difficulty, Mr. G. W. Childs generously paid the first quarter's rent, and on April 1st, 1872, the "Home" was sent forth on its way towards success, with many a prayer offered up by its early supporters.

So far it cannot be said that there was any well devised or definite plan of action.

The only idea which influenced the Committee was that men should be brought into the "Home," be retained there temporarily, be treated as necessity dictated and then sent forth again into the world.

That this idea was carried out by the Committee then in charge is proved by the entries made upon the journal of the house: "John —— came in drunk; stayed all night; got his breakfast and went out." "William —— came in; got a bowl of soup; took the pledge; and went out." "Jacob —— came in; expressed a desire to become a sober man; got supper; took the pledge and was taken to the Ivy and Oak Lodge of Good Templars."

As may readily be imagined, such a
scheme did not afford a very firm basis on
which to build the superstructure of Reformation, and on this account Mr. Godwin
was not satisfied.   His own high aims will
be best described in his own words : " We
design at our Home, by personal kindness
and the love of God, to win back the prodi-
gal ones to the family circle, society, the
marts of trade, and the favor of God, and
to restore them to the image of their Divine
Master."   He, therefore, set himself to
devise some plan which would offer the
greatest possible hope of rescuing men
from a relapse into their vicious habits.
"Personal kindness and the love of God "
was the basis of his action.   To insure the
first, he determined that the domestic life
of the Home should be as encouraging as
it was possible to make it, and for this
purpose he called to his aid an Auxiliary
Board of Lady Managers, composed of
Ladies identified with the various Churches

of Philadelphia; and under their direction the domestic arrangements were thoroughly organized. Previously, things had been very rough, the natural result of the hurry in which the Home had been opened.

The Auxiliary Board of Ladies also undertook the visitation of the families of those inmates who had sunk into poverty through the vice of their head, relieving the distress they too often found there and providing work, when necessary, in the shape of sewing, or some other occupation. Their success is thus described by one of their number, in 1874:

"Through their instrumentality families, long alienated and separated, have been happily brought together. This branch of the ladies' work has been peculiarly blest; and their reward is rich in witnessing not only homes made happier through their labors, but hearts so melted by their personal kindness and by the Gospel message which they carry, that husbands and wives, convicted of the sinfulness of their neglect of the great salvation, come forward to declare themselves soldiers of the Cross and unite with the Christian Church."

The work of this Auxiliary Board of Ladies in the " Home " itself was not less marked, as the words of the First Annual Report, issued on April 1st, 1873, testify :

" The change that followed immediately, in their department, was in such striking contrast to the previous management, as to seem almost miraculous. Their presence was seen and acknowledged at once. Where before had been looseness of deportment, profanity, evil speaking, there was now respect, appreciation and earnest endeavor on the part of the inmates to bear their part in the great work."

Mr. Godwin, thus far, was working out his idea of " personal kindness," but he did not neglect in the slightest degree " the love of God." Daily his voice was to be heard in prayer, in instruction, in earnest pleading with the men. He taught them to look to God, from whom all true and abiding strength comes and Who never fails to bestow it, if approached in penitence and faith.

He had already, together with a number of gentlemen brought by him into the Board of Managers subsequent to the opening of the Home, taken the bold ground that drinking was not a disease in itself, but a sin and sinful habit ; and that getting a man sober was not reformation. To effect reformation, conviction that drunkenness is a sin must be produced ; the will must be made resolute ; a higher, purer, holier standard of morality must be inculcated. Future results will show how effectively these ideas were carried out.

To render the work of the "Home" more practical, it became evident that the Directors and Managers should become a corporate body, and application was therefore made to the Court of Common Pleas of the County, for a charter, which was granted and duly recorded on December

9

11th, 1872, and revised on May 4th, 1874. A difficulty began to present itself very shortly—a difficulty arising out of the success of the early efforts of the organization, or as we may now call it "the Corporation of the Franklin Reformatory Home for Inebriates of Philadelphia." The number of persons seeking admission was in excess of the accommodation of 911 Locust Street. The rooms of that house, although large and airy, were crowded. Persons of means, seeking private rooms, could not have them ; and the accommodation for living and recreation was confined.

Adjoining No. 911 were two houses, Nos. 913 and 915, unoccupied and neglected, known as "the News-Boys' Home." That institution had failed in its object and was at a standstill. "The News-Boys' Home Association" proposed to sell their property to the Franklin Home Corporation, and on January 23d, 1873, less than a year after its foundation, a deed was executed conveying these buildings, 913 and 915 Locust Street to the Corporation, which now became the possessor of a property having a frontage of fifty feet and a depth of one hundred and thirty feet.

Thus an institution of large capacity was secured, but it had not even yet attained the dimensions contemplated by its active President, for five years later he stated in an annual address that :—" The Board expects futurely, by purchase, or otherwise, to increase the capacity of the ' Home,' so as to accommodate one hundred inmates, and can only do so when the general public shall learn (with them) the absolute necessity of such an extension, and the increased good which must result in consequence thereof."

Up to the present moment Mr. Godwin's desire has not been realized. He has left to posterity a legacy of work, perfect, as far as human plans can be perfect, in its methods, its aims and its capacity, but still far from complete in his own estimation.

The Franklin Reformatory Home in January 1873, consisted of Nos. 911, 913, 915, Locust Street and communications between the houses were opened. The whole ground floor of 913 was converted into a chapel, or audience hall, for religious services and meetings ; for every meeting held partakes of a religious character. In 915 an office and conversation room were provided. The rooms in the upper floors were re-arranged, so that small chambers, for one inmate, became available, and the dormitories in general were of such a character that in the majority there were only two beds, in none of them more than four. This system is followed, because it is found that it is advisable for a new inmate to have some one at hand, who can summon assistance in case of necessity.

Provision was also made for infirmaries for those patients who require medical treatment, or for whom seclusion is thought advisable. In 915, as it possessed a large northern projection, a sitting room was furnished, where the inmates could enjoy the use of tobacco, which, in moderation, is never forbidden. Here also a lavatory and bath-rooms were fitted up.

The yards of the three houses were thrown into one, thus forming a courtyard, which in summer is supplied with shrubs and flowers in abundance.

A capacious home having been secured, the Auxiliary Board of Lady-Managers undertook to prepare it for the residence of inmates. Their labors are again best described in their own words :

" Realizing at the time the impossibility, with an impoverished treasury, of purchasing the furniture needed, the ladies undertook the fitting up of the houses by subscriptions from themselves and others. The furniture for our large audience hall was thus obtained, also that for the physician's office and committee room, and some other parts of the house.

"Very recently special exertions have been made to enlist in our needs the active sympathies of the various religious denominations of the city, and with encouraging results. Several churches have consented to undertake the fitting up of the small chambers, each church furnishing a room entire. The Bible Classes of the Episcopal Hospital generously agreed to furnish one room. We thus hope soon to have these apartments in condition for occupancy."

In 1875 the following gratifying statement was made by the same Board of Ladies :

"Since last year's Report, the furnishing of the private rooms has been completed, with the exception of one, for which the bedding and one hundred dollars in money have just been donated by the German and English Lutheran Churches of this city. Other minor improvements have also been added, making the house now what it was originally designed to be, a commodious, well-appointed, cheerful Home for all who fulfil its conditions of admission."

In a similar way the large audience hall, or chapel was completed, and in 1876 the Methodist Episcopal church contributed the furniture of one floor of 911, which was converted into a Reading Room and Library.

It may be said that the Home now stood as it is seen to-day, for there is no necessity to record the various minor changes which have been made, consequent on natural wear and tear. But, as has been already remarked, the accommodation thus supplied for some fifty inmates did not satisfy Mr. Godwin. It remains for the future to show whether his grand scheme will ever be carried out.

In an uninterrupted stream of energy, activity and Christian influence the Home has been at work for seventeen years, until over 4000 inmates have passed through it—men of all stations in life,

all professions, all occupations—passed
through it on the way to reformation. To
quote again Mr. Godwin's earnest and
enthusiastic words :

"The nature of the work is well understood. It is to rescue men from the slavery imposed by intoxicating liquors and
to place those who have fallen in the way
of reformation and (through God's grace)
bring about their salvation. Can the philanthropist be engaged in a nobler object ?
Is there a more charitable work than this ?
From the purest motives the Franklin
Home was instituted. In the face of the
prevalent conviction that the inebriate could
not be redeemed, reformed and restored,
it has demonstrated the contrary by results,
results whose influence has been felt, and
is still making its way, instilling hope into
the bosoms of hundreds of families where
sorrow and sadness yet hold sway."

The work of the "Home" is superintended by a Board of Directors, among
whom have been numbered some of the
most prominent philanthropists of Phila-

delphia. From this Board are elected an Executive Committee, a Finance Committee, and a Committee on Property. For many years the Directors were assisted by the Auxiliary Board of Lady-Managers, whose efforts have already been recorded.

Mr. Godwin presided over the " Home" and the Board of Directors from April 1st, 1872 until his death on February 17th, 1889. Mr. Isaac Welsh was the first Treasurer, and he continued to hold that office until 1887, when affliction compelled him to resign. He did not long survive his resignation, dying on June 2d, 1887. Mr. John B. Love at present acts as Treasurer.

The internal management of the Home is under the supervision of the Executive Committee, of which Mr. James W. Hazlehurst is now the Chairman. One of these, at least, visits the Home every day, to confer about the various matters which may arise, and to arrange about the admission of inmates.

The actual duties of the management are carried out by a Superintendent and a Matron. For several years the Secretary of the Board of Directors acted as Superintendent, and he, being non-resident, was assisted by an Assistant Superintendent.

In the year 1880 a severe crisis came upon the Home, a crisis so severe that the Directors in their Report in April, 1881, said:—" Dark, indeed, were the clouds that overshadowed the Home, on the night of the 10th of June, when the question was asked, '*Must the Home be closed?*' Honest and earnest men felt grieved to think that the noble work the Home was doing might have to be abandoned, but the merciful and good God who had called into life this work, and watched over it, and blessed it, sent down the inspiration that stirred men's hearts to renewed efforts." It was resolved to go on, and the Directors appointed a resident Superintendent who should be responsible to the Executive Committee and through them to the Board of Directors for the conduct of every branch of the economy of the institution. Mr. C. J. Gibbons, who had been connected with the work, except for a short interval, from the foundation of the " Home," was selected for this post, Mrs. Gibbons fulfilling the duties of matron. To his able management the present success of the work is greatly due, and there is not a past or present inmate of the " Home," who will not agree with Mr. Godwin's estimate of their indebtedness to his efforts :

" It would be impossible to exaggerate the obligations of all true friends of the inebriates and of temperance reform to Mr. Gibbons, for his unremitting and successful labors. In the discharge of his exceptionally delicate and exacting duties, he has displayed a rare combination of vigilant zeal, indefatigable effort, minute supervision, intelligent adaptation of means to the end, manly sympathy, Christian forbearance, and steadfast resolution and firmness, which prove him to be specially qualified for the responsible position he has filled with such satisfaction to the Board, and such gratifying results to the unfortunates under his charge."

For the treatment of those who stand in need of medical assistance there is a physician. Dr. R. P. Harris most generously filled this office for ten years, and all who know him are well aware of the deep interest which he has ever taken in the work of reclaiming the victims of intemperance. On his retirement in 1882, Dr. James Graham placed his skill and knowledge at the disposal of the Board of Directors, and long may the Home enjoy the benefit of his generous and able services.

It may be well, at this point, to remove any false impressions as to the true character of the Franklin Reformatory Home. It is in every sense of the word a *home*.

All its surroundings, all its arrangements, all its domestic life, are suggestive of real home life. The dormitories are such as are suitable for men accustomed to all the niceties of the private home. The dining room, with its well laid tables, is a picture of comfort and, in fact, of refinement. The food is abundant, good, wholesome, well-served and fitted for men in any station in life. The library, well carpeted, well supplied with a half a dozen daily papers, and several hundreds of books, well lighted, well furnished, speaks of comfort, as well as of mental improvement. The Chapel, or audience hall, with its benches and chairs, its platform with handsome reading desk and organ, whispers of a higher world than this ; while the motto of the Home, on a framed banner, proclaims the one principle of a " closer walk with God " in this life and the one hope of the Christian for the life to come :—" By the grace of God I am what I am." The conversation room and office, into which the visitor or inmate first enters, speak of the pleasant and encouraging influence which is exercised on all who come within the walls. After a short period there is no offensive restraint whatsoever, each man being at liberty to come and go, under proper restrictions, between breakfast and retirement, by leaving a recording ticket in the rack in the office. The home fulfils its temporal duty by providing every comfort, and trusts for obedience to its rules, for honorable regard for its credit and interests, to the feeling of responsibility engendered in those who enjoy its benefits.

The inmates consist of three classes—those who are able to pay for their board and lodging—those who can only do so partially—and those who are free, the latter class being about 40 per cent. of the number admitted. No distinction is made, all are treated on equal terms and thus mutual support and counsel among all classes of men is stirred up and maintained. The conditions of admission are :

" Persons having a permanent home within the State, whose circumstances render it imperatively necessary, may be admitted to a free bed, at the discretion of the Committee on Admissions.

" To obtain a free bed the applicant, or his friends, must give satisfactory proof of his inability to remunerate the institution for his support during his stay therein.

" All other persons will be charged for their board, according to their ability to pay, and the rooms, attendance and accommodations furnished them.

" No person will be received as an inmate for a less period than two weeks.

" In cases of emergency, applicants may be received temporarily, when they are in proper condition and properly recommended ; but no person shall be considered an inmate, until he has received an order of admission from some member of the Executive Committee on Admissions and Supervision.

" All persons, on becoming inmates, must bind themselves to observe and obey the Rules governing the internal affairs of the Home. Any deliberate violation of them will be considered good cause for removal from the house."

Founded in the way described above, the Home has, year by year, faithfully carried out the purpose for which it was instituted. Up to the present time, the smallest number of inmates admitted in one year was 107, in the first year of its existence; the largest 337, in 1882. The total number of those who have passed through it is 4019, up to April 1st, 1889.

Speaking of the results of the movement in 1885, the truly Christian President showed where the secret of success lay, when he said:

" There is, in fact, more reason than ever before to realize that its labor is Divinely assisted and that in treating drunkenness as a departure from a pure Christian life—the remedy for which departure is a return to Christian teachings and associations—the Home is doing God's work in accordance with His will and wisdom, as results testify."

And those results were mainly due to the spirit, the influence and the energy of Mr. Godwin himself, for, while the development of the Home was proceeding, he was assisting in and practically directing every stage. It would be impossible to put on record every incident which arose from his connection with the Home. For a considerable time he resided in the immediate vicinity and it was no uncommon thing for him to spend an hour or two there, before entering upon his business duties, as well as after his daily work was done. In the early days, before those effectual aids were organized which make it such a success in the present, he might frequently have been seen on his way to Locust street, carrying a half-worn suit of clothes for the use of some poor inmate ; and it may con-

fidently be said that there was no part of
the work which did not receive his closest
attention. One of the Committee, with
whose assistance and under whose supervision this memoir has been prepared, was
admitted to the Home in May, 1872, and
has been closely and intimately connected
with its working and its management all
these years. He therefore knows whereof
he speaks and his words are these :

"There is nothing in the Home to-day
that is good and effective but what was
here the first three months of the Home's
existence, except the Bible study, which
was organized later on. To Mr. Godwin's
brains and unceasing action, moral courage
and generous support in the most critical
part of the Home's life, all the success of
the Franklin Reformatory Home may be
honestly said to be due."

The methods of treating the inmates,
founded on principles of true Christian
Charity and an intimate study of the nature
and character of drunkenness, developed

by wide experience and observation, and
carried out with unfailing tenderness and
persistency are in themselves sufficient to
call for separate chapters.

Standing as we do on the brink of Mr.
Godwin's grave, the words of the last annual address he ever penned for the Report
of the Home seem to have a tinge of pro-
phetic sadness while they ring out a note
of triumph :

" For sixteen years we have battled
against the mistaken judgment of many
well-meaning citizens, our special object
being to establish and perpetuate *a Home*
for alleviating the condition of men who
have become victims of the curse of drunkenness, and now we are able to say, without
equivocation, *the Victory* is ours."

THE GODWIN ASSOCIATION.

———

> " *We pine for kindred natures*
> *To mingle with our own.*"
>> WORDSWORTH.

> " *The craving for sympathy is the boundary line*
> *between joy and sorrow.*"
>> " GUESSES AT TRUTH."

The effect of sympathy, from the day when man found a " help meet for him," has ever been the most sustaining influence in all social relations. That " Union is strength " is well exemplified in the fabled faggot. The whole stood the strength of the strain, while individually the sticks were broken. Sympathy and union will enable men to bear a weight of struggle and temptation, when individual natures left to themselves will succumb.

In no relation of life is this more true than in the struggle against vice, and in the maintenance of Christian sobriety, purity and faith, which are the avowed objects of the Godwin Association of the Franklin Home.

The following history is presented by its Committee on Records as a faithful account of the steps which led to its foundation, of its object, and of its success. Prepared originally in 1883, the Committee see no reason to change any statement, but can only add that the last six years have fully borne out the promise of fruit which the goodly tree of the Association then gave:

"In the month of June, 1872, the Franklin Home, then two months old, had within its walls eleven inmates. By *inmate* is not meant the refuse of society, who used the Home as a temporary refuge, a sort of convenient resting place, where they might recuperate their exhausted bodies and shattered nerves before plunging into renewed dissipation ; nor yet, as a rule, were they applicants for charity. In most instances they were men who had been morally and religiously nurtured, had known the enjoyments of comfortable and respectable homes; while some had even rejoiced in business success, and exulted in the swelling delights of gratified ambition. But in the busy world, where false and dangerous doctrines are insidiously disseminated under the disguise of a so-called philosophy, and morality is too often scoffed at; where the hideous deformity of vice is hidden by trickery of attire; and the Saviour's admonition to 'watch and pray' is either wholly forgotten or utterly neglected; they had trusted in themselves alone and had become involved in the terrible ruin of intemperance.

"But though they had ceased to pray themselves, loving hearts lifted to God earnest supplications for them, and in *His* own good time, God inspired earnest and unselfish men and women to open a door to an ark of safety, where such as earnestly desired to reform, might enjoy the balm of consolation to their wounded souls, and be led to once more look forward with hope and confidence to their future. The Frank-

lin Home was started with an unyielding
faith in God ; earnest prayer and equally
earnest and persistent labor for its success
followed, and men presented themselves,
not to be cured of a disease, but to be
taught how to resist temptation ; to be
turned from the evil way that leads to per-
dition, and to winning back manhood from
the slavery of a degrading habit. However beneficial the influence of the Home
might be to such men, sooner or later they
must again face life with all its difficulties
and temptations, and surrounded by old
companionship and coming into daily contact with pernicious influences, what was
to keep them firm to pledges and resolutions so lately made ? Certainly if love of
wife and children, motives of personal
honor and considerations of policy could
not keep them from falling in the first
place, the memory of benefits conferred
by the Home could not in itself prevent a
return to sin. Indeed, bearing as they did
the wounds and scars of the past, with the
barriers of virtue broken down, familiarized
with evil in its multitudinous forms, they

would naturally succumb more easily to temptation.

"These were the reflections and questions from which emanated the idea of forming an association to which only those who were or had been inmates of the Home should belong, together with the Board of Directors, thus forming a connecting link between the inmates and the Home, that would bind them by the strongest ties; that would happily keep up the influences which had proved so beneficial in the first steps towards reformation, and prevent a renewal of those associations, so pregnant of the evil in the past; that would furnish companions to replace those left behind in the sinful ways of the world ; and by working unitedly within the association for the reclamation of others, occupy the spare time that had hitherto been wasted in dissipation. We would, it was thought, thus secure a powerful influence in strengthening graduates (as those who have passed through the Home are called), and in sustaining ourselves. It has been said that the Association is an auxiliary of the Home,

and it has been asked by men who belong
to that class ever ready and eager to find
fault, but never seeing what is directly
before them ; who are forever asking about
'rights,' but seldom see or perform the
plain duties incumbent upon them, 'Where
does the Association's connection as an
auxiliary begin and end?' So closely are
the Home and Association entwined that
the beginning or ending cannot be found.
Metaphorically speaking, the Godwin Association is the broad, sheltering branches of
a noble tree, whose trunk is the Home, and
whose roots spring from Christian anxiety
to remedy the weakness and alleviate the
misery of fallen men ; or it may be likened
to the thorns on the bush which guard its
beautiful and tender flowers that they may
fill the air with their fragrance. Made up
as the Association is of men banded together in the Spirit of God ; the noble vir-
tues of charity and mercy being its funda-
mental principles ; a firm reliance in God
its only hope and purpose ; its members
seek for no knowledge beyond that which

will enable them to carry out the objects set forth in the preamble to the constitution.

"The credit of organizing the Association belongs wholly to the Inmates of the Home and it must be a source of profound gratification to the Directors and Managers to look back upon the great results for good it has accomplished, recognizing as they must, that it all has sprung from their own noble, disinterested charity and fidelity to Christian principles."

In the early part of June those of the eleven inmates, who were interested, consulted Mr. Godwin, who expressed approval of the scheme and promised his support.

"A formal meeting was held June 20th, 1872, at which eight persons were present. The meeting was opened with earnest prayer to God for His blessing and protection by Mr. Samuel P. Godwin, President of the Home."

One of those present at that meeting remembers that Mr. Godwin demurred to the proposal that the Association should bear his name, but, by a ruse, he was induced to leave the room, and on his return the name, "The Godwin Association of the Franklin Home," had been unanimously adopted. Temporary officers were chosen and a committee was appointed to prepare a Constitution. In July, a Constitution was submitted and adopted—the following preamble to which clearly explains the objects of the organization.

" PREAMBLE :—We whose names are hereunto subscribed, having experienced the blessings and benefits that emanate from the ' Franklin Home,' and believing that they have been directed by God's Providence, and knowing that there is no better or more pleasing way to evince our gratitude to our Heavenly Father for His favors and mercies than to aid our suffering and erring fellow creatures, hereby agree to form an Association, having for its object mutual assistance, and the reclamation of our fallen brethren, and adopt

for our government the following Constitution."

The First Article of the Constitution
goes on to say :

" The object of the Association shall be
to bind ourselves together by social intercourse and brotherly interest for each
other, so as to effectually promote the purpose for which the ' Franklin Home' was
instituted, and to render mutual assistance
at all times to our fallen brethren and by
every means in our power to resist and
oppose the use of, and traffic in intoxicating liquors."

The pledge taken by each member on
being elected into the Association, and renewed by the whole body at the weekly
meeting is as follows :

"We whose names are hereunto subscribed do solemnly promise to abstain
from the use or sale of all spirituous, or
malt liquors, wine, or cider, and that we
will not provide them as an article of entertainment, neither will we offer them to

our associates, or provide them for persons in our employ.

" We also pledge ourselves that we will, under all circumstances, discountenance their use, God being our helper."

The officers of the Association are the President, Vice-President, Secretary, Assistant Secretary, Treasurer and Chaplain.

" The Constitution having been adopted the Association became a living, active auxiliary to the Home, besides being to each and every one of us an additional safeguard. After progressing about one month, it became evident that in order to hold together, we must be up and doing. The idea of taking under its charge a bed in the Home was broached and immediately acted upon, and in addition, voluntary subscriptions were received to defray expenses and Standing Committees were appointed as follows :

Committee on Home ;
Committee to visit sick members;
Committee on entertainment ;
Committee on Records.

" The Committee on Home has charge
of the beds of the Association, and the relief of any member in distress.   If this
Committee hears of any member being so
unfortunate as again to fall into evil habits,
it immediately hunts up the fallen one and
persuades him to return to the Home.
When, as is generally the case, there is no
member requiring the good offices of the
Committee, any one is received who can
be reached, the only requirement being a
sincere desire for reformation.   By this
Committee much good has been accomplished and many men have been saved,
who otherwise would have continued in
their downward course until spiritual, as
well as physical death, had overtaken them.
In addition to this, if a member is in pecuniary difficulty he receives the brotherly attentions of this Committee.

" The committee to visit sick members
has charge of the sick, sees to their wants
and watches over them.   It visits those
members who do not attend the meetings
of the organization, and, generally, works

with and in conjunction with the Committee on Home.

" The Committee on Entertainment has charge of the Tuesday and Thursday night meetings. The good resulting from the work of this Committee must be evident to all who are familiar with those meetings.

" The Committee on Records has charge of what might be termed the history of the organization.

" With this organization the Association has worked for seventeen years—always in unison and harmony with the direction and management of the Home.

" We look back and ask ourselves what have we achieved during the past seventeen years ; what have we to show for our expenditure of energy, time and money ? And the satisfactory and gratifying answer is—look at the number of members occupying positions of trust, men in business, men at the mechanic's bench, men in the laborer's garb, humble, yet honorable. These are the monuments that to-day give the lie to the theory that intemperance is a disease, and that reformation is impossible.

"We can point to families where once the returning footsteps of the husband and father were heard with fear and trembling ; where only the sobbing of a broken-hearted wife, mingled with the wail of innocent and suffering children, disturbed the dread silence of a desolate home.   But now that the demon of intemperance is banished, with its attendant discord, want and tears, and the Spirit of God and Religion with the Angels of Peace and Happiness are enthroned, there may be heard the click of the sewing machine, running in unison with the quick and joyous heart-beats of the happy wife, who, anxious to aid her reclaimed and recovered husband, spends the time formerly devoted to sobbing and mourning, in helping him in his struggles with life, while little children await with loving anxiety the approach of that father whom erstwhile they dreaded, and the mother, by the clear and merry laugh, as it rings out, as only innocent and happy laughter can ring, *knows he is coming*.

" We can point to homes where wealth and refinement had brought together all the evidences of culture and luxury; where statuary and paintings studded and adorned the frescoed walls ; where rare exotics mingled their sweet perfumes with the songs of birds hanging in gilded cages, but where, as you entered, the very air seemed to whisper, ' Hell's black viper has been here,' while in the prematurely old and careworn face of the wife, the uplifted and fear-expectant faces of the children, who knew no happy childhood hours, you might read the sad, sad story of intemperance that is always the same in palace or hovel —always the same. The gorgeous surroundings of these palatial residences but served to mock the heart of the wife, who waiting the return of the ' erring one' falls asleep only to ' dream of coming woe.' But now all has changed ; the gilded shackles which bound the wealthy inebriate have been broken ; the husband has been reached ; false-hearted and dangerous companionships have been severed ; the man was, for the time being, taken out of his own hands, introduced into new and good company, and, after physical strength had been restored, the murky clouds of false and delusive theories cleared from his mind ; his heart warmed again with all its generous emotions, and with a soul overflowing with gratitude to God, the husband and father has been returned to that luxurious residence, and in the general happiness and joy a new beauty is given to what before was not merely a brilliant, but a hideous mockery.

" It may be asked, have we only joy and happiness to look back upon ? We answer, 'No!' We have many cases of perverseness on the part of some of our members ; ingratitude on the part of others. Men who, under the Providence of God, have been rescued, have again fallen away, owing to causes which are easily found. They have attempted to sustain themselves by a pledge and association alone. This cannot be done. These are merely human means and help. To God alone must we look for strength and grace to make all these things efficacious.

" The novel and practical feature of the working part of the organization is the absence of any secrecy, oaths, badges, regalia, initiation fees and weekly dues. The contributions are entirely free-will offerings from honest men who desire to aid other men. The money is used to assist needy members, either by a donation or a loan, and in paying the expenses of two beds in the Home.

" It will thus be seen that, with the Committees thoroughly organized and earnestly working, this Association is what is claimed for it—a great auxiliary of the Home's work.

" The Association, however, is not merely an auxiliary to the Home, but the two are mutual and effective supports, the one of the other. If there is one quality more than another that marks its history, it is the perfect unity and absolute harmony that prevails. True, some men have left us, complaining and dissatisfied; but that is the best evidence of unity, of our sincerity of intention and action. There are men who recognize in the noble work of the

Home ; in the self-sacrificing devotion of
the Directors ; nothing but a field in which
to play the hypocrite and practice fraud ;
and to add to the chances of success, they
join the Association.   Here, however, they
are expected to practice, as well as preach,
the lessons of wisdom and virtue taught in
the Home.   We are practical men ; our
knowledge of life, its deceptions and vices,
has cost us years of woe.   We played the
fearful game ; we staked character, happiness, prosperity and everything which
made life desirable, but from the bitter
experience gathered we have gained a
knowledge of life, enabling us to recognize
the ring of true metal, so that when precon-
certed deception or hypocrisy is attempted
here, when the best feelings of our nature
are being outraged, something, under Divine Providence, occurs to expose the fraud
and protect the holy interests of the Home
and the Association.   Gold and debased
currency will not circulate together ; so here
sincerity of intention, earnestness of purpose and integrity of action will not har-
monize with mere professions.   Hence,

insincere men will leave us complaining of
something or some one; the loss is theirs,
not ours.

"Let us who remain be true to the
Home and the Association which have
brought us so much peace and happiness.
Let our aim be so to improve and extend
our Association in its sphere of usefulness
and love, as to develop and utilize its fullest
capacity for Christian work. Let us hand
it down to the men who are to follow us,
with its name unsullied and unchanged.
This is our high resolve, and, God willing,
we shall keep it. Our object is to make
the Association a monument of our gratitude to the Home, which will live after
those who are now active in the holy work
have been called from this world of care,
to enjoy everlasting bliss."

These words were placed on the Records
of the Godwin Association in April, 1883.
In February, 1889, one of the band of
workers went, indeed, "from this world of
care, to enjoy everlasting bliss." Of him
the Report above quoted says:

" The President of the Home has frequently said he is proud of the Association
—he has reason to be, for when he has
passed away ; when in the lapse of years,
his personality shall have been forgotten ;
his children's children will point to the
Godwin Association as an evidence of his
humanity, Christian charity and assiduity
in originating and developing it, as a means
for the advancement and improvement of
his fellow-men.

" To him, the President of the Home
and the Association, no words can adequately express our gratitude. In joy or
in sorrow he has ever been the same to us.
It has been truly said, the Franklin Reformatory Home is a family. To every
family there must be a Head, and to the
family of the Franklin Reformatory Home,
Samuel P. Godwin is the father, whose
every thought and action is for the benefit
of his children—asking no return, but that
he may see them regenerated, happy men,
worthily filling their proper places in life."

The meetings of the Association are held
on Tuesday evening and Thursday evening,

at eight o'clock, as well as on Sunday afternoon at three and Sunday evening at eight,
in the chapel of the Home.

The Tuesday evening meeting is one of
mutual counsel, relation of experience, instruction and entertainment.

The one held on Thursday is for the
transaction of the business of the Association, the election of new members and discussion concerning anything connected with
the welfare of the body. On Sunday afternoon a Bible Study is held, and on Sunday
evening a service conducted by some Minister from among the various Religious
Bodies of the city.

All the meetings on Tuesdays and Sundays are open to the public, and at each
of the meetings through the week Prayer
is offered up and Hymns are sung; for, as
before stated, the Association holds that
nothing can be attained in the way of
reformation, unless Divine grace assists

the efforts of their body, as well as those
of each individual.

The Association is not a merely theo-
retical support and auxiliary of the Home,
as is shown by the fact that it regularly
supports two beds in the institution, that it
has in addition to this given, in nine years,
upwards of $9500 towards its maintenance,
as well as providing additional comfort by
bearing the expense connected with replen-
ishing articles of furniture and lighting.

The value placed on the efforts of the
Association by the Executive Committee
of the Home may be stated in the words
of their Fourteenth Annual Report:

" We feel impelled to speak more at
length of the operations of the Godwin
Association than we have in the past. The
members of the Association have been
especially active and their work satisfactory in the highest degree. They have
contributed $420 for the board of inmates
who were brought to the Home by the
Visiting Committee of the Association.

Hundreds of men have been redeemed by
the efforts of those who have themselves
experienced the benefits of the Home.
Never have the Thursday night meetings
been so well attended as during the past
year. Your Committee feel assured that
to these meetings much of our success is
due. Attendance upon them is a privilege
that few appreciate at its true worth. So
potent is their influence that we have never
known a member, regular in his attendance, to fall back into the ways from which
he had been rescued. The graduate who
is for any reason unable to attend these
meetings, is bereft of the most powerful
weapon to fight against his own evil inclinations. We do not say that one who wil-
fully absents himself from these meetings
will fall again, but we do say that the
probabilities of his remaining steadfast are
greatly diminished."

And once more. The Superintendent
of the Home, Mr. C. J. Gibbons, has said :

" It is poor praise of the Godwin Association to say that it is as noble a brother-

hood as ever battled for the good of human kind and that before long its work will be felt as no work in the same direction was ever felt before. It is growing every day in strength, and when its energies shall have been massed, it will be known, from one end of the country to the other, as one of the most powerful organizations of its kind ever brought into existence. The course of the Godwin Association is well worth watching."

In a later report still the Superintendent speaks even more enthusiastically :

"In the work of protecting the harvest which the Home has garnered, the Godwin Association is of inestimable value. It is the army of occupation in the citadel captured for God ; it is the imperial guard of the treasures recovered from the enemy ; it is the grand army of the republic of virtue which, while it wears laurels for past victories, continues in active service ; it is a veteran association formed on the field and staying on the field, without pay or pension."

The Godwin Association indeed may be called the back-bone of the Institution. An hour rarely passes, on any day, without some member visiting the Home; using it' in fact, as a club house, enjoying the society of the library, the smoking and conversation rooms, and entering into encouraging talk with any present inmate.

As a still further proof of what the Association does to keep its members true to their principles, their pledges, and their God, the following words of the Seventeenth Annual Report, presented by Mr. Gibbons, will be read with deep interest:

"After the primary reformation of drinking men and their induction into the Godwin Association, there is no phase of the Home's system more valuable in itself, and more worthy of receiving attention, than its plan of gathering on holidays and days of marked public excitement all of its children. In the very first year of the establishment of the Home, the managers, knowing the characteristic ebullitions of the drinking habit on the Fourth of July, and though not lacking faith in the stability of their graduates, determined to stand between them and possible danger, by calling them all to the Home on that day, and in the evening giving an entertainment for them and their families followed by refreshments.   This was done and was the commencement of the extended system since adhered to.   It must be apparent to the most superficial that it was a wise idea ; that a man would very likely go home drunk from Gloucester, or after parading the streets, and that he would very likely go home sober in the company of his family and after a day and evening spent in the House in which he found his salvation from drunkenness, and among those who under the grace of God saved him and those who were saved with him.   Thus on election days, when citizens exercise the God-given right of voting, of approving by their ballots existing laws, or protesting against them ; when, by a perversion of the intention to surround the exercise of suffrage with sobriety and virtue, drunkenness, noise

and confusion reign and a predisposition
to crime is engendered, the Home realizes
the danger and again calls in its graduates.
They spend the afternoon at the house, an
oyster supper is served which will compare
favorably with anything of the kind served
by the best caterers, and in the evening a
meeting is held to which the wives of the
inmates and graduates are invited. On
his way homeward after the meeting, the
man is not likely to go yelling and hur-
rahing through the streets and perhaps
spend the night in the station house.

"Like the sober citizen he is, he gathers
his news with his breakfast the next morning, from authoritative sources and goes
quietly to his business as on any other day.

"Thanksgiving Day is the next public
holiday in which the Home sees dangerous
temptation; the very day set apart for a
free people to thank God for the blessings
of liberty and prosperity. And it is on
this day that the sinks of iniquity and
fountains of crime make special prepara-
tions to receive their guests, hold out the
extra inducements of lunches and music to

entice men to go to them and *be happy*,
save the mark ! The climax of indecency
and diabolism in satire has been reached
when, with the consent of society and the
sanction of law, men are asked to get
drunk, and risk damning their souls by
way of thanking God for His goodness to
them ; when they are deliberately asked to
recognize the bounteousness of the Creator
by prostituting that bounty to the vilest of
purposes ; when, instead of soberly praising God for the reason He gave them, they
undo the reason and supplant it with
violent madness or drivelling idiocy. That
none of its own may be even scandalized
by this monstrous profanation, the Home
has its inmates and graduates within its
walls, a Thanksgiving dinner is spread and
enjoyed ; and in the evening at the meeting it is not difficult to see that the reformed men of the Home realize that
thanks given to God can only be given
with an unclouded mind, and that there is
no freedom so sweet as freedom from sin
and habit that enslaves.

"It is a harsh criticism on the social

customs of a Christian people, that the eve of the anniversary of the birth of Christ should be celebrated with bacchanalian songs, ribald jest, profanity and riotousness ; that the birthday of the Redeemer should be ushered in with profane conduct in direct contradiction to everything He taught, and the example of His whole life be set at naught. On this holiday too, does the man whom the law selects to minister to the people's vice, contrive enticements to degradation, and as he contemplates his ribbon-bedecked turkey he complacently rubs his hands and invites his guests to make for themselves a happy Christmas. The jingle of glasses and rattle of dice invade the quiet of the street, and the day that should be one of orderly religious joy, becomes a saturnalia of sin. Again the Home interferes to avert the danger. The night before Christmas it entertains its graduates and inmates, their wives and children, and Christmas Eve is always a notable night. A Christmas tree is prepared laden with presents which the generosity of the manufacturers and mer-

chants of the city have bestowed, enabling
the Home to make a Happy Christmas for
so many. Not every man who has reformed springs at a leap from poverty to
even comparative affluence, and if the
kindly contributors to this festival at the
Home could see the happiness they make,
they would find themselves more than re-
paid for their liberality. Articles of usefulness, wearing apparel, toys, candies and
fruits are distributed, and there is joy in
many a family which on former Christmas
Eves, with a drunken father rattling dice
in a tavern, were sorrowful enough to
make a sympathetic heart throb in anguish.

"On New Year's Eve the Home is again
found making a diversion from the scan-
dalous customs which are a blot on Christian civilization. On the last day of the
year, when it would seem natural that men
should pass in review the year nearing its
end and form high resolves for the year
so soon to begin, we find the occasion used
as though it was fitting that the evil of the
year should culminate in riotous dissipation ; a pandemonium round a death-bed.

On this night the Home once more calls
to its children and gathers them in. The
night is consecrated to serious reflections
on the deeds of the dying year, to the
inspiration of holy ambition for the year
to come. There is a lecture, religious
services and a sermon by one of the ministers of the city. After this, during an
intermission, refreshments are served and
the last hour is devoted to meditation,
thanks to God for His goodness to mankind, prayer and hymns of praise. Riotous
revelry fills the streets ; within the Home
there is profound peace. As midnight
draws near and every passing moment
brings the old year nearer to a close, the
congregation falls on its knees and in
silence sends up to the Father petitions for
strength and wisdom to do all and be all
that they have resolved to be. As the bells
sound the dirge of the old year and the
welcome to the new, their voices peal out
too, and ' Praise God from whom all blessings flow,' rings through the chapel and
far out into the night air, sweet and per-
vading as incense, sung from the heart by
men and women whose knowledge of sor-

12

row has taught them what true joy is.
Then there is a reunion such as few places
know as the Home sees it.

"The man who goes home with his wife
and children after this, is not going to stop
anywhere and buy a bottle of whiskey to
finish the night with or get drunk on the
morrow.

"It must be noted that these entertain-
ments to divert men's minds from temptations of the time do not make any inroad
on the Home's general fund. They are
taken care of by generous friends acting
through the officers of the Home. Nor
must it be understood that they are attended only by the poorer graduates and
inmates. Graduates of the Franklin Home
are proud of it, rich or poor, and while
some are necessitous and the entertain-
ments are a boon to them, many leave luxurious homes to be with us and testify by
their presence the salutary influence of the
institution."

How such enthusiasm is generated in the
men who have passed through the Home
to swell the ranks of the Godwin Association will be seen in the following chapters.

THE METHODS OF THE HOME.

I.

The Medical Method.

" Pars sanitatis velle sanari fuit."

SENECA.

It was part of the cure to wish to be cured.

No words can so adequately, so simply and completely describe the medical meth ods pursued in the Home, in reforming the drunkard, as those of the able Physician, Dr. R. P. Harris, who, for ten years, gave his services to this work. Those words are here reprinted from the Annual Reports of the Franklin Home.

In one of these Dr. Harris says :

" In presenting my Sixth Annual Report, permit me, in commencing, to congratulate you on the continued prosperity of the

Home, its growing usefulness, and the increase of confidence manifested in it by the community around us, which, slow to believe at first, is gradually becoming more and more convinced, that there is such a thing as a permanent and reliable reformation. The longer the probation, the greater becomes the confidence of a doubter in the feasibility of the plan adopted, worked out, and tested in the Institution which you have in charge; and when we shall have doubled our age, we may hope for a corresponding measure of faith in the possibility of a complete reformation.

"The question is frequently asked of us: 'Do you really think there is such a thing as a thorough reform?' And when I mention the fact that A has stood firmly for four years; B, for five; and C for nearly six, I am answered: 'This is very encouraging, but men will drink after a longer interval than these.' I am then forced to draw from an experience much older than the Home, and relate cases that, under Christian faith and influence, have stood through trials and temptations for much longer periods, even up to forty years, without failing. I have had patients that reformed years ago, and died in the faith, after many years of probation; and I could point to the living, whose day of trial has been many times that of the oldest graduate of the Franklin Home. Two of my patients, long since gone to rest, were, under God, the means of reforming one who has also been under my care, whose years of temperance nearly double the age at which he ceased to drink. This form of argument generally closes the question of possibility to the satisfaction of the inquirer.

"The disease theory of inebriety, so much written about during the last ten years, has done more to shake the faith of the community in the possibility of reform than anything that has been advanced upon the question of Temperance. To cure the disease and destroy the drink-craving, so that it will stay cured, are the great desiderata in the opinion of those who advocate and those who believe in this theory. In the Franklin Home, and

in the Washingtonian, of Chicago, this
theory is not advocated or believed in ; and
there are no persons so opposed to it as
those who were once drunkards and are
now reformed men. This drink-craving,
so often given as an excuse for breaking
faith, is not believed in by our reformed
men, who, with rare exceptions, declare
that the desire for drink never troubles
them, as long as they do not taste it, or
put themselves in the way of the various
forms of temptation which lead to a social
glass. This step taken, no matter how
long the interval may be, at once excites
an irresistible desire for an *ad libitum*
measure. If this is a fact, then the treatment of inebriety, after the few days required to remove the effects of the alcohol
from the nervous system and digestive
organs, is simply educational and moral.
As a general rule, it requires but a short
time to restore a drunkard to health.
There are exceptional cases, but the great
majority have ravenous appetites in a few
days, and soon report themselves as feeling better than they have felt for some

months, or even years. The insatiable thirst for alcohol so soon departs that we are usually able to give a man his liberty to go and come, with safety, at the end of a week.

"The medical work, except in cases of *mania potu*, insanity, and ruined constitutions, is soon over with the newly arrived inmate, and then the work of teaching him to reform, and how to remain so, is commenced by the inmates, graduates, and all connected with the Home, who feel an interest in its success. It is often a slow, uncertain, and discouraging work; but the failures are as nothing when weighed with the many bright examples of success which are gradually swelling the ranks of the little army of reformed men, whose influence will be felt as a power in this city at some future day, when their number shall enable them to organize for aggressive work, as has been done in Chicago, where the Home has been much longer in operation.

"If association inclines men to take a social glass, the Home affords them a companionship that is not opposed to this kind of sociability. If fond of company, and time hangs heavy on their hands, here is plenty of entertainment in the form of books to read, games, social conversation and evening meetings, with speeches, music, and other kinds of diversion. There is no greater power for good or evil in the land than that of association; and as it makes most of the drunkenness, so when wisely and properly directed under Christian influence it may be made to undo some of the evil that has been done by the very elements that, under a different influence, never wrought aught but ruin. There is no influence that weighs so much with the inebriate as that of the reformed and truly converted graduate of the Home. Nothing encourages a man so much, when truly desiring to reform, as to compare notes with a reformed man whose case resembles his own and learn from him how the great change was brought about."

We now approach the actual treatment of the persons who become inmates of the

Home. With regard to general treatment, Dr. Harris says :

"The inmate at his entrance is at once deprived of all intoxicating drinks. He generally shakes very much and seldom sleeps well the first night. He takes remedies to calm his system, improve his appetite and make him sleep, which is generally accomplished by the second night. He is well fed, washed, shaved, and made as presentable as possible, and becomes quite steady by the third or fourth day, and so changed in appearance, that in many instances, the marks of intemperance are not noticeable, and he can scarcely be recognized as the drunkard of four days previously. I have almost entirely abandoned the old system of treating intemperance and delirium tremens, being enabled to do this by the use of valuable remedies recently introduced into medicine, and known to the profession generally. I have abolished altogether the *tapering off* treatment, as well as the use of hop tea *ad libitum ;* as the former is not required, and the latter is only an excuse for ·drinking as a medicine, what is virtually a substitute for, and leads to the use of something stronger.

" As soon as a patient has a good appetite, and sleeps well, unless he has a tendency to diarrhœa, or some other malady, I stop all medicine, as its use only tends to make the inmate regard himself too much in the light of a patient, when he should have his thoughts upon reformation, a resumption of honorable employment and leading a new life. Many of the inmates at the time of their admission, have lived almost entirely without food from one to three days, during which time they have been almost continuously intoxicated; and strange as it may seem, but very few of them run any risk of *delirium tremens* by being suddenly deprived of all stimulant, provided they can be made to eat and sleep, which is generally easily accomplished.

"As drunkards become such under very different exciting causes, so they require very different methods of treatment, and offer every grade of prospect as to ultimate curative results. This is of great importance to be borne in mind, when we are limited in resources and, at the same time, desirous to accomplish with our means the greatest amount of good. The case of the confirmed and habitual drunkard is, as a general rule, more hopeful than that of one who for several months, or years, has no desire for drink, and then becomes suddenly seized with an inordinate passion even before he has tasted it. Some drink from fondness of taste, others from a desired effect, or to drown care, &c.; and some I have met with, who hated both taste and smell, and yet drank to a fearful excess at long intervals, owing to a peculiar nervous organization. In the great mass of cases, there is an association of taste with effect; and the power of the will, which is weak before the first glass is swallowed, becomes a rope of sand, as soon as the influence of this drink is experienced. Our great effort is to be expended in the prevention of the taking of this first drink, and in strengthening the will to resist all forms of inducement, whether mental or extraneous, to resume the habit.

"Natural impulse and moral associations have a great deal to do with creating a taste for drink. We hear much of the inheritance of intemperate habits ; and this is often given as an excuse for the indulgence by the second generation ; but is not this very much exaggerated? It is difficult to separate this idea of inheritance from the effect of example at home ; and no doubt the evil of the latter is, in many instances, the commencing inducement with the children. We have certainly seen families, whose fathers, fortunately for them, did not live long enough to pollute them by their example, where the whole moral training of a good mother, appeared to have eradicated all traces of any supposed hereditary taint. Some men are fortunately constituted with a perfect command over their appetites, lasting through life ; some lose this power and become drunkards in old age ; and others have an innate fondness for liquor, which only reveals itself at the first indulgence, generally on this occasion leading them to drink to intoxication. Other subjects are the un-

fortunate possessors of a peculiar nervous
organization from childhood up, which
renders them liable to indescribable attacks
of agitation of the nervous system, which
are at first under the control of alcohol,
but require, for their continued suppres-
sion, larger and larger potations, until the
amount consumed is, in some instances,
marvellously great. We have had such a
case at the Franklin Home, and there did
appear at one time, strong ground for
hoping that he might be permanently
reformed; but after numerous trials and
relapses, we were obliged to abandon all
further attempts as hopeless. With many
of this type, the habit is only occasional,
and with some, at very long intervals,
varying in one of my patients from two to
seven years. Any unusual cause of depression, whether of sickness or otherwise,
may bring on a desire to drink, which at
other times is entirely absent, requiring no
exercise of will for restraint. He says
that he has no desire whatever for drink
when he is not indulging, except under the
peculiar impression referred to, and dis-

likes the smell and taste of whiskey so
much, that he has often held his nose
whilst drinking, to avoid them. When
indulging, he usually drinks to such an
excess, that I have known his pulse to fall
to forty beats per minute, after three days
of intemperance. It is this class of cases,
which more closely in their nature resem-
ble attacks of disease, and yet there are no
true evidences of a malady, until the party
said to be afflicted, gives way to his inclination to drink.

"The infirmary erected at my request,
enabled me to inaugurate a rigid temporary
seclusion of every man admitted under the
influence of alcoholic stimulants, or who
has been up to a very short period using
them to excess. This plan was adopted
and put in force for several reasons, and
the result has not only justified my decision,
but fully met the expectations indulged in
at the time that past experience forced me
to make the experiment. The importance
of the plan can be best understood when
I state what is effected by it. An inebriate deprived suddenly of his accustomed

stimulant, especially when this has been indulged in to great excess, runs a considerable risk of being seized with delirium tremens, in from one to three or four days; and this result is very much to be dreaded and anticipated, if the man at his admission is found to have a rapid, feeble pulse, trembling hands, and a weak stomach. To avoid this result must be the first endeavor in his treatment; and to do this, if possible, without resorting to the old system of *tapering off*, a plan which happily is only now requisite in but one type of cases, which, as our institution is not a hospital, it is our duty to exclude as far as possible, on the ground that the experience of the past teaches us, that few such cases enter with any sincere desire for permanent reformation.

" After the first effects of a debauch are passing off, the inmate becomes nervous, restless, fearfully thirsty ; cannot sleep, or dreams very much if he does; and if the occasion offers, will escape to get a *drink ;* or will use cold water to great excess ; smoke and chew tobacco in the same degree, and ultimately become so sick at the stomach, that the plan of his restoration is defeated, by reason of his inability to take nourishing food, and he throws himself into the disease which it is his and our interests to avoid.

"To remedy these enumerated ills, the plan of shutting up each inmate, when required, was adopted. This prevents all chance of escape, whilst his craving for alcohol is most active ; prevents his making himself inordinately sick at the stomach, by drinking, as a majority will, from half a gallon to a gallon of cold water in a day ; keeps him from the use of tobacco, enables me to use such remedies to best advantage, as will quiet nausea, allay nervousness and produce sleep ; and permits of the employ-ment of highly nutritious diet upon which must mainly rest our hopes of rapidly over-coming the effects of alcohol in its power of enfeebling the whole physical nature, and keeping up a craving appetite which it is almost impossible to control."

"We rarely find it necessary to shut up an inmate for a longer time than three days,

and have in very few instances, even in
mania potu had a case under lock and key
beyond the seventh day, and seldom on the
fourth. It is also astonishing how quickly
the thirst for whiskey leaves the large
majority of inmates when treated without
it, and under a belief that the best permanent physical restoratives come from the
provision dealer rather than the apothe-
cary."

" We are also becoming more than ever
convinced that it was a fallacy which in former years led physicians to resort to the
use of stimulants, gradually reduced in
quantity, in the treatment of inebriates
placed under their care after a debauch,
fearing that a sudden cessation would necessarily result in an attack of mania. Sickness of stomach and diarrhœa, but particularly the latter, are far more dangerous to
the recently admitted inmate, than the sudden stoppage of his accustomed drink,
which is of no consequence to him, provided his strength can be restored by sleep
and food. One inmate who was apparently in excellent condition on the third

day, was suddenly seized with a severe and obstinate diarrhœa, which in a few hours so exhausted him, that mania set in, which was not entirely removed for four weeks, or until the diarrhœa had long been arrested, and the physical strength restored by nutritious food. In such cases, the mental condition varies with the changes in physical strength from day to day, and every little improvement or drawback in the latter, is shown by corresponding changes in the former, until at length the strength of body is evinced by an ability to keep the mind in balance through all the waking hours.

"We care very little, in a medical sense, how long or how much a man has been drinking, provided he has been able to eat so as to keep up a reasonable degree of flesh and strength, or can be made to sleep and eat within twenty-four or thirty-six hours after his admission. We have treated men by sudden total abstinence who have drank a quart of whiskey daily for a year, and had no difficulty in restoring them to a very fair condition in a few days; and we have seen mania develop itself in those who had drank much less, and for a much shorter period, simply because they were exhausted for want of proper food, and could not by reason of nausea, loss of appetite, or diarrhœa be properly nourished. What benefit there can be in the use of alcohol, which has been the cause of this disability, we are at a loss to determine. What we have to fear in many cases is death by congestion of the brain, a condition which is certainly favored by alcoholic treatment.

"We have seen very marked benefit from an unlimited use of milk in some cases, where the mind was such that no solid food would be taken. We have repeatedly tested and compared the alcoholic and abstinent methods of treatment, and from at one time a frequent resort to brandy, have gradually come to a point where it is a questionable matter whether we cannot, in all instances, attain better results without alcoholic stimulants than with them. We have certainly had some remarkable recoveries from *mania potu* in exhausted, broken-down subjects, where not a drop of alcohol was used, and have failed in similar cases, repeatedly, in former years, where brandy was freely administered."

Later on, Dr. Harris writes:

" Having had over one thousand inebriates under my care in the past seven years, I have fully tested the nutritive and stimulating plans of treating inebriety and alcoholic mania, and am satisfied of the value which food possesses over alcohol, particularly in cases of extreme exhaustion threatening death, from which we have had several marvellous recoveries in the Home, one of them during the past year. This case reached its maximum of danger at one of my night visits, on which occasion I made the remark to the Assistant Superintendent, that I had repeatedly lost such cases in hospital, under the old alcoholic treatment, and that I could not see the philosophy of continuing the use of stimulants, where it was so evident that they, and the want of nourishing food, had produced the existing prostration. I therefore directed him to give the patient all the milk and strong beef-tea he could get him to swallow, at short intervals, until I should see him in the morning. At the morning visit there was an improvement, and he slowly recovered strength, being restored, finally, from a condition of *dementia*, threatening permanent insanity, in about a month ; he is now in business and in very good health."

Dr. James Graham, who succeeded Dr. Harris in 1882, says of his experience during that year :

"In only one out of the one hundred and twenty-six cases were alcoholic stimulants administered, yet they all recovered, and, I believe, in as short a time as if alcohol had been used. The exceptional case, not recovering promptly, milk punch was given and apparently with benefit. Especial attention was directed to the prevention of the development of *delirium tremens*, and the superior quality of the food, its rich abundance, and the devotion of my assistants, undoubtedly shielded many a poor sufferer from that horrible disease.

"We may fairly conclude that in mild cases at least and under proper treatment, it is absolutely safe, and eminently desirable, for the drunkard, at once, and without preparation, to renounce all intoxicating drinks; and where a proper diet and faithful nursing can be procured, instead of precipitating himself into delirium tremens, he, by so doing, in an incredibly short time recovers his lost manhood."

Speaking of the dangers of alcohol, Dr. Graham says:

"Our usual plan of treatment is to dispense with all alcoholic stimulants, but in no cases, not even the most severe have we given the usual alcoholic drinks, brandy, wine, &c., but have found that alcohol medicated in various ways gives us the desired temporary stimulation without keeping alive morbid tastes.

"Many drinking men believe the only danger their habit exposes them to is that of *delirium tremens;* but this is a grave mistake; only the few have delirium tremens; but many, very many, meet death

from other diseases that are directly or in-
directly caused by alcohol. If mortuary
statistics told the truth, the public would be
startled at the vast number of deaths from
alcoholism; but this insidious poison deceives, even in death; for the doctor, to
spare the feelings of the relatives and the
memory of the dead, reports the case as
of one Bright's disease, liver disease, heart
or brain disease, when it should be alcoholism. Or if, as in this case (one of pneumonia), the *disease* is not directly caused
by the poison, the *death* is; for had he not
been an inebriate, the same amount of exposure would, probably, not have caused
the pneumonia, or had he contracted a
similar disease, he would almost certainly
have recovered."

The same authority says:

"We are frequently told by patients in
the infirmaries, that it is not the whiskey
they drank that has injured them, for they
were accustomed to that 'all their lives;'
and that it was only when they had drifted
down into the slums and imbibed the

' poisonous, doctored stuff,' which was sold there, that mind and body had become diseased. This is an error that many of their more favored brethren believe in, but *the* poison of strong drink, whether the cheapest that is sold in the lowest dens of the city, or the purest that comes from the best distillery is *alcohol;* the adulterants used are almost invariably harmless, and the more it is diluted, the less injurious it becomes, so that prince and pauper are poisoned by the same ingredient, only the effects are retarded by abundant food and good hygienic surroundings in the one, and hastened by starvation and exposure in the other."

Unfortunately the hurry of life, with its harvest of shaken nerves, has led many persons, who would revolt from the ordinary interpretation of drunkenness, to have recourse to various drugs which have a similar sustaining or soothing result for the time. The results may be described as intemperance, equally with the use of alcoholic liquors. Moral, mental, social

degradation are the effects in both cases.
It is therefore with gratitude that the following words of Dr. Graham should be
studied :

"There is an increased proportion of
cases that are addicted to the use of other
drugs than alcohol, and I fear this proportion will alarmingly increase, if the medical
profession do not hide their medicines behind their Latin formula. It is highly re-
prehensible for a physician to advise his
patient to take so much morphia, chloral,
or bromide, whether for the relief of pain,
to procure sleep, or to ward off the effects
of alcohol ; for the man finds that it not
only relieves his distress, but gives him
pleasant sensations as well ; and the next
time he goes on a debauch, being ashamed
to consult his physician, he gets the remedies without his advice, and then dis-
covers that he can get drunk on one drug
and sober up on another, and by and by
he reverses the order and gets drunk on
the chloral, and sobers up on the whiskey.
The double dose accomplishes its final re-

sult with double speed and with doubly
direful results, and often leaves a wreck
that drifts helplessly and hopelessly into
an insane asylum.   The physician should
order his alcoholics with the same secrecy,
for there is no more reason why a sick
child should know that it is taking whiskey
in its milk than it should be told there is
calomel in its powders.   As alcohol is
mostly used for a temporary effect, when
the patient recovers, any relief he may
have experienced was caused by a, to him,
unknown drug.   As an illustration I will
cite the case of a man, a devoted father,
strongly opposed to the use of alcoholic
drinks and holding an esteemed position in
his Church, and society.   He was ordered
by his physician to take paregoric and ginger for a chronic diarrhœa ; it had a favor-
able effect on his sickness but, continuing
its use, he developed a taste for it and increased the dose until he took, for months,
upwards of a pint of paregoric in a day.
The remedy then caused other diseases
and unfitted him for business and he was
driven to the use of whiskey to counteract

its effects. Realizing his danger he made frequent vain efforts to break his shackles and at length he came to the Home, where after a dangerous illness he finally recovered."

This chapter cannot be ended in a better way than by quoting once more the suggestive words of Dr. Graham :

"Among the readmission cases, a common story is as follows ; the man had abstained from all alcoholic drinks for a series of months or years, until, from some cause, feeling in poor health and unfitted for his usual work, he had a craving for a stimulant ; but acknowledging to himself the great danger he would run in taking a single drink of whiskey, or beer, he deceives or excuses himself by drinking essence of ginger, or one of the many bitters that are in the market, and which contain alcohol ; and once the morbid appetite is gratified, reason and manhood are stifled and he commences a reckless debauch. The moral of this tale is, that the reformed drunkard should keep his

general health in the best possible condition, avoid excessive fatigue, and, if he feels
sick, consult at once his family physician,
tell him truthfully his past history and get
a safe remedy to tide him over his danger;
or if he does not think that the case needs
a doctor, let him be fully aware that, though
the taste for alcohol be disguised, yet its
effects will promptly tear the mask away,
and it would be more honest and less dangerous for him, to drink plain whiskey,
than the alcohol under another name; but
fortunately there are non-alcoholic drinks,
that to a man, under a stress of work or
worry, will afford the desired relief—a
bowl of well-spiced beef tea, a glass of
milk, or a cup of coffee or tea, will yield
the wished-for assistance much better, as
well as much more safely, than the bever-
ages dispensed in the bar-room, or drug
store, and it will be advisable for the wife
and mother to know this, as well as the
reformed inebriate."

If success be a standard by which theories and practice ought to be judged, Dr.
Harris and Dr. Graham may claim the

highest success ; and their theory and practice, in following out Mr. Godwin's idea,
may well be recommended to the consideration of that noblest of human professions, in which skill and knowledge are
combined for the purpose of alleviating
the misery and suffering of mankind.

THE METHODS OF THE HOME.

II.

THE SUPERINTENDENT'S VIEWS.

" More helpful than all wisdom is one draught of simple human pity that will not forsake us."
                                        GEORGE ELIOT.

The Superintendent of the Franklin Home, Mr. C. J. Gibbons, having been engaged in the work of the Institution almost ever since its foundation, must be regarded as one qualified to speak with authority. His views are well illustrated by the following extracts from his annual Reports:

." One of the great difficulties to be encountered in the work is the wrong impression many persons have of the Home and its object. Some suppose that they have to pick up every wretched man they

meet and bring him here and that we are
to receive him without knowing anything
whatever of him, or his antecedents. Others
believe the Home to be something between
an Almshouse and a Hospital, to which
men may be brought to receive medical
treatment for the effects of drunkenness,
or, as they express it, '*to straighten a man
up.*' This is a gross misconception. The
Home was founded, and has been kept up,
to aid men who seek permanent reformation, not to help those who merely wish to
'*get off a spree.*' Others again are disposed to treat the Home simply as a sort
of hotel or boarding-house in which liquor
is not sold ; a notion fatal to the influences
it desires to exercise.

"The best way to dispose of these and
other erroneous views is to give a detailed
account of the workings of the Home, and
explain its method of dealing with the
cases that present themselves for treatment.

"The man whom drink has driven to
the shelter of the Home, usually enters it
with but vague ideas and purposes of

reformation. He is broken down physically and mentally, he has worn out the
patience and alienated the affections of his
family and friends, he is not unfrequently
embarrassed also pecuniarily, and worst of
all, is broken in spirit and without hope
that he will be able to break the fetters
that render him the unwilling slave of alcohol. This being his condition, the first
thing done is to quiet the disordered nerves
and excoriated stomach and to remove the
physical maladies produced by excessive
drink. Skilful medical treatment and careful nursing generally bring the patient in
a few days to an approximately healthy
condition, though time is necessary for his
complete restoration to vigorous health.

"The next step is to extend to him sympathy and encouragement, to rekindle a
spark of hope in his lacerated heart. He
is made to feel that, however abandoned
his condition, there are still those who care
for him and feel an interest in his welfare,
and who are ready to extend to him the
hand of help and brotherly kindness. He
feels assured of the possibility of success

in his attempt to reform, when looking at the encouraging example of those around him—his fellow inmates. His most pressing wants are relieved, and if the necessities of his family trouble him, his mind is made easy in regard to them. If, as is sadly too often the case, his vicious life has separated him from wife and children, steps are taken to heal the breach, if possible, and reunite him to his family. Where it can be done (though our power in this direction is necessarily limited), he is aided in obtaining employment, and stimulated to get at work, to regain that confidence and respect in the community which he has forfeited by his habits of dissipation.

"Strengthened and supported in this manner, almost any man, however weak, can be kept away from liquor for a time, and it is during this period of sobriety, when the reason begins to resume its sway, and the prospect of a new and happier life is opened up, that the work of laying the foundation for a permanent reformation is begun.

"The man is made to realize that he is

a drunkard, he is taught to seek out the causes that led him to become one, and every effort is made to convince him that total abstinence is his only safety, and that a single drink means ruin. It is also made plain to him that a return to his old associates and modes of living will lead him again to drunkenness, and that he must henceforth live another and a better life, with different aims and surroundings.

"The central teaching of the Home is that drunkenness is a sin, and that the only way of escape is by repentance and faith in God's divine promises of grace and help to resist temptation.

"We have no confidence in the permanence of any reformation that is not based upon sincere religious convictions and sense of duty. A radical change of heart is necessary, and we know of no other means by which that change can be effected. The drunkard to be rescued must be born anew to fresh hopes, to higher aspirations, to purer tastes, and to holier desires. We do not hesitate to employ, in proper subordination, human aids

and motives ; but the aim of all our efforts
is to bring our erring and fallen brother
humbly, earnestly, and with sincerity of
purpose, to seek and accept Divine assistance. And we believe that when this is
honestly and intelligently done, no attempt
at reformation need be a failure.

"Brought to a true sense of his condition, made to realize both his own weakness and his own strength, educated into
a correct understanding of the circumstances affecting his life, and taught to
rely upon the only true source of aid and
comfort, the reformed man must begin to
take again his place in the world, to face
temptation, and to build among the broken
fragments of a ruined past the noble fabric
of a reformed life. But to succeed in this
he still needs help. It is not sufficient to
merely point him to the right path, and to
place his staggering feet upon the thresh-
old ; we must bear him company for a time,
and see him fairly started on his onward
and upward journey.

"This object is accomplished through
the Godwin Association, a society for mu-

tual aid and improvement, composed of
the present and former inmates of the
Home, and holding its meetings weekly
in our chapel. Every two weeks, those
new inmates who give sufficient evidence
of an intention to reform, are presented
for admission as members. After being
addressed by the President, in earnest and
stirring words of admonition, encouragement, and sympathy, they covenant to
Total Abstinence—not in the blind heat
of a spasmodic remorse, but after having
had ample time for deliberation, and proper
instruction as to what the pledge means,
and what is necessary to enable them to
keep it. The general objects of the Association are, to keep its members under
the influence of the Home after they cease
to be inmates, to enable us to follow them
up and look after them, by visiting and
correspondence, and to afford opportunity
for mutual aid and counsel.

"It is but right to add, that to the co-
operative assistance thus obtained, the
Home owes a large measure of its practical success. Under the auspices of the

Association are held weekly, on Tuesday
nights, Conversational Temperance Meetings. These meetings play an important
part in carrying on the work of the Home.
The audience is, for the most part, made
up of the present and former inmates, with
their families and friends. Short, earnest
addresses are made on temperance topics,
and the reformed men tell their experience of the curse of drink and its cure.
These 'experiences' do not consist in gloat-
ing over the foul picture of the man's previous degradation, in rolling each repulsive
circumstance of it as a sweet morsel under
the tongue, to pander to a morbid, mawkish
taste. Nor do they recount a drunkard's
struggles with a resistless appetite that
never existed, save in his diseased imagina-
tion, as I shall endeavor to explain further
on. They are simple narratives, setting forth,
in homely, but effective phrases, the causes
and the effects of drunkenness, and the
means and method of its cure, as understood by the management and inmates of
the Home. These meetings are at once
the school of instruction for new inmates,

and the voice by which the Home speaks to the public and spreads its influence abroad.

"Special religious instruction is provided by the Sunday afternoon Bible Studies, conducted by Mr. Samuel P. Godwin, the President of the Home, and by the Sunday night services. These services are unsectarian, and are conducted by clergymen from the pulpits of the various denominations in the city. They are of such a character that Christians of every shade of opinion may join in them with pleasure and profit, and without hearing their own views called into question. Relying wholly as we do upon God's help for effecting reformation, we lay the greatest stress upon this portion of our labor, striving to make this institution, in every respect, what it professes to be, a *Christian Home.*

"From what I have said of the Home and its methods of work, it will be seen that we make no profession of being able to reform men against, or without the co-operation of their own will, either by restraint, or so-called 'scientific treatment.'

Nor do we teach the dangerous and irreligious doctrine that a man can conquer the habit of drink merely by the exercise of his will. But we maintain, that every man, however abject his slavery to drink, can, with God's help, reform, and lead a sober life, and we profess our readiness to stand by him, and aid him in making the effort.

" One of the chief difficulties with which the inebriate has to contend, both in overcoming the habit and in extricating himself from the miseries in which it has plunged him, is the almost universal disbelief in the possibility of reforming a drunkard. A man cannot put his whole strength into an effort, unless he himself believes that he has some chance of success, and it is a serious discouragement to him to feel that those about him think his task a hopeless one. This is the common impression with regard to the attempt to reform, and is the natural consequence of the belief that drunkenness is a 'disease,' and is caused by an 'appetite,' practically irresistible and existing independently of the stimulus it receives from alcoholic drinks. This 'disease and appetite' theory the Home rejects, although by no means surprised that it is so generally received.

"There exists to justify it the notorious failure of many mistaken methods of cure, and the sad example of so many impotent attempts to reform ; and, owing to the almost criminal facility with which pledges are administered, and taken by wholesale, an immense number of pledged men relapse, which leads the world to think that it is only a question of time when those who still stand will fall again. We are told by some influential medical and scientific men that drunkenness is a disease, that there exists, or may be generated, a practically uncontrollable physical appetite for drink, which never dies. This serves as an apparent explanation of the facts, and seems to warrant the conclusion that when a man has once become the slave of drink his fetters are rivetted on for life. Fortunately it is not true. Drunkenness as a 'disease' —that is, a disordered condition of the system, independent of the will of the patient

—does not 'exist, except in those who by prolonged or excessive use of alcoholic poisons have brought the brain into the condition that may be produced by a blow of a loaded bludgeon, and who are recognized as wholly or partly insane. It is even safe to say, that, used in its right sense, there is no such thing as an appetite for strong drink. Those who use alcohol to excess are conscious of a feeling of 'craving' in their disordered stomachs, which may generally, though not always, be temporarily allayed by stimulants; but it may safely be asserted that this craving does not exist in those who have never used liquor, or who have given it up, and been restored to health.

"This is the point at which the Home has left the new track of worldly theories, and taken the beaten track of divine truth in grappling with the vice of intemperance and its inseparable evils. The Home has never denied the fact that there may be physical causes predisposing the man to drink which he may be unable to resist if not fortified with Divine grace; nor does

it deny that a man becomes morally and
physically diseased by the use of liquor,
and that having once created within himself a physical and mental inclination to
drink, he is forever after weak in that direction. But, while the Home admits all this,
it denies positively that on that account the
man *must* at times drink, *must* get drunk,
and *must* finally die a drunkard.

  " But how, it may be asked, can we explain the return to drink of men apparently
reformed, who have a clear knowledge of
the power of the habit, and the unutterable
miseries it brings in its train? Our experience has taught us that in each individual case it is by no means difficult to assign
a sufficient reason, though it may not be
easy to give one that would cover all.
Sometimes it is because the man has no
means of amusement and recreation except
those connected with the drinking customs
of society. He takes part again in the
various forms of social intercourse with a
firm resolution not to drink; but the force
of habit and old associations, and the soli-
citations of friends, are too strong for him,

and, when the first glass is taken, all is over
for the victim of the vice. Others lack the
moral courage to face the trials and difficulties of life, and find it easier to drown
in liquor their conscience and their sense
of duty, than to comply with their stern
requirements. Nothing is more common ·
than this. A man finds himself broken in
health, purse and spirits, and the forgetful-
ness and temporary happiness offered by
the wine cup prove an irresistible temptation. There are some whose tastes and
feelings have been so vitiated and depraved
by long years of dissipation that they con-
stantly long for the excitement and grosser
pleasures of intoxication, and in an hour
of weakness they yield to the tempter.

"When due allowance is made for these
and other moral and mental causes, it will
be seen that the reformed man falls, not so
much because of the cravings of a physical
appetite, as because he has thrown away
the safeguards that were holding him up,
and keeping him sober. He goes again
among the temptations of life, forgetful of
the admonition of the Saviour of the world

to "watch and pray." In such cases the
man has never really reformed—he failed
to accept the principles and be guided by
the teachings of the Home. We do not
count him among our failures. Even in
his interval of sobriety he was wedded at
heart to the sin of intemperance, and was
sure to fall back, sooner or later, into that
gulf from which there is, humanly speaking,
no means of escape, where the victim of
sin is so tormented by its sufferings that
his sad state appeals not so much to our
indignation as our pity.

"What the condition of a confirmed
drunkard is we know but two well. His
nerves are tremulous and his whole body
diseased ; his reason is clouded, his will
enfeebled, and his moral sensibility dulled
and depraved. Over all his past hangs a
black shadow of remorse, projecting itself
into a future unilluminated by a ray of
hope. It is at this stage, when, whatever
his social status, be he rich or poor, ignorant or educated, he is a physical, mental
and moral wreck, that the Home raises the
fallen man with one hand, and lifting the

other to Heaven for help, proclaims the possibility of his reformation, and asserts the essential worth and dignity of that nature which was created in the image of God. However wretched and degraded the individual, we believe that in him there still lingers some spark of the Divine fire, which if he will lend himself to the effort may be fanned into a purifying, vivifying flame. And our experience justifies our faith and fills us with hope for the future."

THE METHODS OF THE HOME.

III.

Religious Influence.

" Serve God before the world: let Him not go
Until thou hast a blessing ; then resigne
The whole unto Him ; and remember who
Prevailed by wrestling ere the sun did shine.
Pour oyle upon the stones ; weep for thy sin ;
Then journey on, and have an eye to heaven."
VAUGHAN.

As soon as the inmate's reason is re-stored, God is pointed out to him as the true physician of the soul.   He is made to understand that reformation is a dual work, a work of Divine grace and human effort; that in the retirement of his own chamber he must ask God for the grace to view himself as he is, and the past as it was.   In his examination he must be sincere and thorough, seeking no excuses, but honestly

acknowledging the cause of his misery.
He will then see that habits, weak as cob-
webs in the beginning, become strong as
cables, dragging him down without the
power to resist, because he never sought
it where alone it can be found; or if the
whisperings of conscience and the stings of
remorse would sometimes warn him, he
went on unheeding, trusting to his own
perverted reason and weakened will that
he might escape the consequences of his
course, although the road he was travelling
was filled with men ruined by indulging in
the same vice. But the time for reflection
has come at last; he cannot get away from
facts; he has entered into himself and sees
his true condition, and is ready to adopt
any remedy that will bring him peace of
heart, strength of will and strength of body.
This is the first step in the man's reformation, the knowledge of his own weakness
and the desire for a remedy.

He is now ready to listen to the invita-

tion of mercy given to the poor sinner.
"Come unto me, all ye that labor and are
heavy laden, and I will give you rest," has a
new meaning to him. "Though your sins
be as scarlet, they shall be as white as
snow," opens to him the hope of forgiveness. The Good Shepherd leaving the
ninety and nine sheep to search for the lost
one is an assurance of loving kindness, if
he throws himself into the arms of Jesus
with a trusting confidence in His goodness,
an abiding faith in His power, and with an
earnest and sincere intention to change
his whole life, and in the future to live according to the laws of God, which he now
finds will secure his happiness in this world
as well as in the next.

Few men hear these teachings without
being impressed, in a greater or less degree,
and in most cases they are influenced by
them; they find them to be the only
anchor on which they can rest their future
safety.

Every inmate attends the Sunday afternoon Bible Study, conducted, until his
death, by the President, Mr. Godwin, where
he hears the great Christian truths enun-
ciated and applied to the vice which has
made the Franklin Reformatory Home a
necessity. Mr. Godwin's long experience
and sympathetic nature, added to his quick
perception and clear judgment, enabled
him to distinguish between the sin and the
sinner ; and while he condemned, with
just severity, the one, he encouraged, with
words of kindness, the other, and pointed
out the only path which can lead to an
honorable and happy future.

On every Sunday evening there is a
service in the chapel of the Home, where
men of every shade of religious opinion
meet ; the reclaimed and the reclaimer
kneel as creatures before one common
Father, the God of all, to offer their praise
and thanksgiving, to supplicate pardon and

mercy for past sins, and beg for grace against future temptations.

Clergymen from different churches officiate.

Those who have felt and appreciated the power and beauty of a religious service can well understand the holy and healing influence, which this bending before the footstool must have upon men who had indeed "fallen among robbers," but now find themselves among the good Samaritans who are binding up the wounds of soul and body. Here is met all that is holy and reverential, all that is encouraging and soothing, and heads learn to bend in prayer which never bowed before, and voices take up the sweet songs of Zion which rarely, if ever before, had sung words of innocence and purity.

Mr. Godwin's peculiar power was never seen so much to perfection as on Sunday afternoon. Earnest, magnetic one may say, as he was on all occasions, his whole soul seemed stirred within him, as he explained and illustrated some passage of Holy Scripture, and drew forcible lessons applicable to the condition of those who sat before him, lessons enforced in all sincerity and truth, while conveying unspeakable love and sympathy.

The following is given as a specimen, one out of very many, chosen only because, while it illustrates the character of the Bible Studies, it was the last which he ever delivered:

"NAAMAN THE LEPER.

"'Now Naaman captain of the host of the king of Syria, was a great man with his master and honorable, because by him the Lord had given deliverance unto Syria: he was also a mighty man in valor; but he was a leper.'—2 Kings v: 1.

"Naaman, the Syrian, was an Aramite warrior, and this remarkable incident in his life, which has been preserved to us through his connection with the prophet Elisha, is found in the 5th chapter of the Second Book of Kings.

"It is said that Naaman was the archer

who drew his bow 'at a venture,' and with
his arrow struck Ahab with his mortal
wound, thus giving 'deliverance unto
Syria.' He had killed one who was not
only the enemy of Syria, but of Jehovah
as well, and this had given him great position in the court of Benhadad. He was
commander-in-chief of the army, and was,
consequently, nearest the person of the
king, whom he accompanied officially, and
supported, when he went to worship in the
temple of Rimmon. He was afflicted with
leprosy of the white kind, which had hitherto defied cure.

"Such was the man, in brief, who *in his
own way*, sought relief at the hands of
Elisha, and who, as the sequel proves,
found it from Elisha in another way.

"What does earthly greatness afford
after all? A man may be ever so popular,
he may be carried upward and onward in
the world's estimation and in gratification
of his selfish ambition, until he has reached
the very acme of popularity; he may climb
the highest pinnacle of political preferment,
or military greatness; may be considered

as the great man of the age; the com-
mander and chief of the affections of the
people; or, like the great Cæsar, he may
hold in his hand the heart of the multitude;
he may achieve wonders by the bow and
arrow of his courage and talent in over-
throwing the chief enemy of the nation's
best good, and even by both pen and
sword conquer the enemies of the Lord
Jehovah and yet, like Naaman, be a leper.
For man, whatever his position in this
world, if he be out of Christ, is a sinner,
and that spoils all, making every cup of
his life bitter.

"Leprosy was incurable and spread
itself until the whole body was bloated,
disfigured, filthy. Oh, wretched picture of
man's mind, his lost condition through sin!
And what is still worse, like the leper, he
finds every effort to cure himself is vain.
How many know the truth of this conclusion! How they have labored and studied
to cure themselves of their defilement!
How many have tried will-power, the force
of argument, the eloquence of worldly
wisdom, and still the leprosy has remained!

Oh, how loathsome is sin! How we have longed to get better and how invariably has the disease fastened upon us, making us worse than we were before the effort was made!

"There was not a physician in all Syria, who could cure Naaman. If such could have been found, money, honor and glory would have been thrown at his feet. My brother friend, there has never yet been found any remedy on earth for sin. The wisest have tried to find the philosopher's stone, but have always failed. Search all nations: man has found no cure for sin. The world is one great leper-house; and God hath chosen the weak things of this world to confound the wise, to propose the remedy, the balm that heals.

"A little captive maid is God's messenger to the mighty Syrian Naaman, through his wife. Hear her when she says, 'Would God, my lord were with the prophet which is in Samaria! for he would recover him of his leprosy.' And with the captive maiden we say to you, my brother, in all the love of our nature sanctified by God's

Holy Spirit, 'Would God you were at the feet of Jesus this day and He would cleanse you from the leprosy of sin !'   None other can.   There is no remedy to be found for the defilement of that sin which has brought you here, no surety for your future safety, unless you go to that greater Prophet of the New Jerusalem, for He alone can cure you of your leprosy.

"The King of Israel had no such faith as this little girl ; he only thought the Syrians sought a quarrel.   Lost, wrapped up in himself, as a great King, he said, 'Am I God, to kill and to make alive, that this man doth send unto me to recover a man of his leprosy?'   But it was not so with Elisha, the servant of God ; for when he heard that Naaman sought relief, he sent for the leper to come to him. 'So Naaman came,' and so like man was his way of coming—with gifts, horses and chariots ! 'And he stood at the door,' expecting Elisha to receive his gifts, but Elisha received none of them, for the salvation of God is not bought with gold and silver and chariots ; it is a free gift 'without money and without price.' Oh that men could learn this !

" And Elisha sent a messenger unto him say, 'Go and wash in Jordan seven times, and thy flesh shall come again to thee, and thou shalt be clean.' Elisha does not come out to Naaman : he sends a messenger to him. What of this ? Why, my brother, it teaches us that it must be by faith, not by sight, not by a sign. God simply gives us His word. 'He that believeth shall be saved,' not he that waits for sight or sign, after the Gospel promises and commands, but he that believeth.

" My brother, Jordan was the type or figure of death. The ark had stood there while all Israel passed over dry shod into the land of Canaan. Oh, what a striking illustration of Jesus taking our place in the river of death ! There was no cure for this leper but to be dipped seven times in the river of death. There is no means on God's earth, as we most conscientiously know, by which a sinner can be cleansed, but by the death of Jesus. 'His blood alone cleanseth from all sin.'

"The leper became very angry at the suggestion of such means to cleanse *him*, the great man, the king's right hand man, from leprosy. Oh! how the human heart rebels against God's manner of dealing, against His mode of cleansing from sin! Surely, the leper thought, there would be some great thing done to him, some wonderful effort and ostentation necessary, something different from the simple proposition of Elisha. And so with the sinner. Surely, he thinks, God must do something to me, or in me, by which I shall be saved. 'Burial in Jordan!' Why this is contemptible. To die to self and thus be made alive in Christ. Impossible! Ridiculous! I will have none of it. 'Besides, are not Abana and Pharpar, rivers of Damascus, better than all the waters of Israel? May I not wash in them and be clean? and he went away in a rage.' What poor sinner is saying in His presence to-day 'Are not my own views, sustained by human reason, better than this free salvation through the death of Christ alone? My wisdom, my beau-ideal of knowledge, my inclinations tell me that it is better to wash in the rivers of my own religion of human reason and moral action, than simply to believe God about the death of Christ.'

" Well; try, try hard, and your experience will be that of hundreds of others, my brother.   Wash, wash in your own 'rivers of Abana and Pharpar,' the rivers of your own 'Damascus,' and, with millions of others, you will be forced at last to admit that the leprosy still remains.   How many from this ' Home' have found in darkness, sadness and misery this fact ; how many have found this ' Home,' with all the leprosy of sin upon them, after trying their own waters of 'Abana and Pharpar ' and yet have continued to refuse the 'waters of Jordan,' and go forth from its walls with the leprosy still clinging to them, even unto death !

" Have you ever known a man whose sins were forgiven by washing in any other waters than the crimson stream which flows from the City of God ?   No, no, there is not one who washes in other water, who either does, or ever can know, that he is saved.

"Naaman's servants say, ' My father, if the prophet had bid thee do some great thing would'st thou not have done it? how much rather then, when he saith to thee, Wash and be clean?' How much better to accept than to reject, if ever so trivial in our view, how much better to admit than to cavil! ' Then went he down and dipped himself seven times in Jordan, according to the saying of the man of God, and his flesh came again like unto the flesh of a little child, and he was clean.'

"How beautiful this picture of death and resurrection—the two great lessons of God! The death of Christ—the end of sin ; the resurrection of Christ—the beginning of an entirely new existence. The old leper goes down into death, buried with Christ—the new man comes out in all the freshness of a new-born child spotlessly clean in his new creation. ' And he was clean.' This is God's only way of cleansing—' In the body of his flesh through death, to present you holy and unblame-

able and unreprovable in his sight ' (Col.
i : 22). Jesus went down into death.
Every believer is dead with Him, buried
with Him, risen with Him, saved through
Him, without spot or wrinkle or any
such thing (Rom. vi ; Eph. v). This is
the source of true, practical life. Oh ! to
know the power of the resurrection ! being
made comformable to His death !   to leave
poor, sinful, leprous self in Jordan ! In the
grave of sin !   This is the great lesson to
be learned.   Often when we think we have
learned it, we discover we have to go
deeper into it.

"Are we still occupied with the old
leprosy, remembering ' the wounds and
the bruises and putrifying sores ?' Down,
down, in Jordan is our place.   Down,
down in death is the only place for self.
Buried there, we rise in Christ.

"Let us look away to-day from the old
leper to the risen Christ. If in Adam we
are full of the poison of sin, God hath made
the risen Christ to be our wisdom, sancti-
fication, righteousness, and redemption.
There is no leprosy in the risen Christ.

So if we have gone down into the Jordan of His death and left our leprosy there, then we are now 'every whit whole,' for we are risen with Christ, and in Christ, and ' there is now no more condemnation.'

"Have we all learned this wondrous lesson, my brethren, wonderful in its simplicity, glorious in its realization? Hast thou gone down into death and risen with Christ? Then 'set thy affections on things above where Christ sitteth at the right hand of God' (Col. iii: 1). Every oil spot of leprous sin is gone.

"'If any man be in Christ, he is a new creature; old things are passed away; behold all things have become new.'

"'And all things are of God, who hath reconciled us to himself by Jesus Christ, and hath given to us the ministry of reconciliation ;'

"'To wit, that God was in Christ, reconciling the world unto himself, not imputing their trespasses unto them; and hath committed unto us the word of reconciliation.'

"'Now then we are ambassadors for Christ, as though God did beseech you by us : we pray you in Christ's stead, be ye reconciled to God.'

" 'For he hath made him to be sin for us, who knew no sin ; that we might be made the righteous of God in him (2 Cor. v : 17–21).

"In conclusion ; I have a good and glorious message for you to-day, dear brother. It seems almost too good to be true. Yet it is the word of God. You have only to go down into Jordan by faith, for Jesus Christ hath borne your griefs and carried your sorrows, and so received upon Himself your iniquity, the whole penalty of your sins. That is extinguished in His blood ; and you are forever free from the leprosy of sin—if you only believe it.

" It is done. It is complete. Provided only that you will believe and accept the announcement. It is not a matter of merit, work, worthiness, or anything in us, that goes before, accompanies, or follows after, but it is given us absolutely for nothing ; simply to believe and accept.

" Jesus says now to every one of you, 'Son, be of good cheer, thy sins be for-

given thee;' and whosoever hath faith to
take that word from Christ is dead to self,
alive in Christ, and is forgiven. You are
living beneath your privilege, and fail to
make use of your prerogative, if you do
not believe this. This security is the com-
pleteness of your Saviour's work. Believe,
and the leprosy of sin is gone and is as
dead as the pursuing hosts of Pharaoh
after the Red Sea closed upon them.

"The great distinguishing characteristic
blessedness of our Christian Revelation
is, that the guilty, helpless, undone, leprous
sinner need only let all else go, and con-
fide in Jesus, and all his sins are covered
and for ever swallowed up in Christ's
atoning blood.

"As God's ambassador, sent to you this
day, I declare to you His forgiveness in
Christ Jesus, and entreat you to embrace
and enjoy it. Do you believe? Do you
now believe? It is not concerning the
forgiveness that we inquire, brother; but
whether you believe? The forgiveness is
already perfect to every one that believeth.
It is as sure as the resurrection of Christ,

and equally sure whether we feel it or not.

" Brother, does your heart ache within you when thinking of all your sins and follies ?   I have a precious word for you.   It is the word of your loving Lord and Saviour: 'Son, be of good cheer; thy sins be forgiven thee.'   And just as thou believest that word, so it is unto thee.

"Oh the preciousness of the glorious Gospel of the blessed God?"

Can it be wondered at that men, under such teaching, found the strength necessary for reformation ?   Will any one dare to say that they distrust reformed men brought to a better life under such influence?   Can the world be surprised when those who have found true peace of mind, true rest on God's promises and grace from the teachings of Samuel P. Godwin and his "Franklin Home," mourn over his loss in the words of the Psalmist king: "Very pleasant hast thou been to me: thy love to me was wonderful, passing the love of women?"

THE EASTER BIBLE STUDY.

"Yea, though I walk through the valley of the shadow of death, I will fear no evil.—Psalm xxiii : 4.

The following Bible study must also be added, as being characteristic of Mr. Godwin, as well as a favorite one with the members of the Godwin Association:

"But now is Christ risen from the dead."—1 Cor. xv: 20.

" The fact of Christ's resurrection is well attested beyond a 'peradventure.' It is needful that it should be beyond dispute, since it lies at the very basis of our holy faith. It is consoling to think that it is so, for thus our foundation standeth most secure and most impregnable. Our Lord was careful to show Himself after His resurrection to those who, having known Him before His decease, would be able, unflinchingly, to answer for the identity of

16

His person, so as to dispel all doubt and cavil in the future. To put the matter beyond all controversy, He took special care to appear many times and to numerous companies. St. Paul gives a summary of those appearances which had most fully come under his own notice :

" ' He was seen of Cephas, then of the twelve ; after that he was seen of above five hundred brethren at once ; of whom the greater part remain unto this present, but some are fallen asleep. After that He was seen of James, then of all the apostles. And last of all He was seen of me also, as one born out of due time.'

" From the evangelists' report we are lead to believe that Christ appeared no less than twelve times, to His disciples ; for some of these instances which the Apostle Paul mentions under one head may include two or three appearances ; as, for instance, 'then of the twelve' may denote His two visits to the Apostles ; for you remember that He first appeared to them when Thomas was absent, and afterwards when Thomas was present. Isaac

Ambrose gives a summary of these appearances to this effect—He showed Himself to Mary Magdalen apart, then to all the Maries, next to Simon Peter alone, afterwards to the two disciples journeying to Emmaus ; to the ten Apostles, when the doors were shut ; to all the disciples when Thomas was with them ; to Peter, John and others when fishing in the Lake of Tiberias ; to five hundred brethren at once ; to James, the Lord's brother ; to the eleven disciples in Galilee ; to all the Apostles and disciples at Olivet before His Ascension ; and last to the Apostle Paul on the road to Damascus.

"There may even have been more than these, for we have no proof that all His appearances are on record. Enough, however, we have, and more would answer no useful end.

"So clear is the evidence of Christ's resurrection, that when Gilbert West, a celebrated infidel, selected this subject as the point of attack, and, filled with prejudice, sat down to weigh the evidence, and to digest the whole matter, he was so star-

tled with the abundant witness to the truth
of the fact, that he expressed himself a
convert, and has left us, as a heritage to
the Church, a most valuable treatise, entitled 'Observations on the Resurrection of
Christ.' He went to the subject as though
he had been a lawyer examining the 'pros
and cons' of any matter in dispute, and
looked at in this way, that which is the funda-
mental doctrine of our faith, seemed to him
so exceedingly clear, that he renounced his
unbelief, and became a professor of Christianity.

"Does it not strike you that very many
events of the greatest importance recorded
in history, and generally believed, could
not, in the nature of things, have been
witnessed by one-tenth as many as the
resurrection of Christ?

"For instance, the signing of famous
treaties affecting nations, the birth of
princes, the remarks of Presidents and
Cabinet ministers, the projects of con-
spirators, the deeds of assassins; any, and
all these, have been made turning points
in history, and are never questioned as

facts, although but few could have been present to witness them. The most recent political event, whether in convention or mass-meeting, I venture to assert, had not nearly so many witnesses as the resurrection of Christ, and, if it came to a matter of dispute, it would be far easier to prove that Christ is risen, than to prove that Washington, Lincoln, or Garfield are dead. If it came to the counting of the witnesses who saw either of them die, and who could attest the identity of the body, when resting in the vault, with that which they saw fever-stricken in the bed-chamber, it strikes me that they would turn out to be fewer than those who saw the Lord after He had risen, and were persuaded that it was Jesus of Nazareth who was crucified, and then burst the bonds of death.

"If this fact is to be denied, there is an end of all witness, and we may say, deliberately, what David once said in haste, 'All men are liars,' and, from this day forth, every man must become so sceptical of his neighbor that he will never believe anything which he has not seen himself, or, equally absurd, never believe anything which he cannot understand. The next step will be to doubt the evidences of his own senses; and to what further follies men may rush, I will not venture to predict.

"We believe that the very best attested fact in history is the resurrection of Christ. Historical doubt concerning the existence of Napoleon Bonaparte, or the stabbing of Julius Cæsar, or the Norman Conquest, or the assassination of Lincoln and Garfield, would be quite as reasonable as doubt concerning the resurrection of the Lord Jesus. None of these matters have such witnesses as those who testify of Him—witnesses who manifestly are truthful, since they suffered for their testimony, most of them dying an ignominious and painful death on account of their belief. We have far more and better evidence for this fact than for anything else which is written in history, either sacred or profane.

"Oh! how should we rejoice, we who hang our salvation wholly upon Christ, that, beyond doubt it is established, that 'Now is Christ risen from the dead.'

"The representations of the context, we take it, are twofold. Death is here compared to sleep; 'The first fruits of them that slept.' But you will, moreover, plainly perceive that it is also compared to a sowing; for Christ is pictured as being 'the first fruits.' Now to obtain a harvest there must have been a sowing. If the resurrection of Christ be 'the first fruits,' then the resurrection of believers must be looked upon as a harvest, and death would, therefore, be symbolized by sowing.

"*First*, then, we have before us the picture, so commonly employed in Scripture, of death as a sleep. Let us not make a mistake by imagining that *the soul* sleeps. The soul undergoes no purgatorial purification, or preparation slumber, in the limbo of the fathers; beyond a doubt, 'To-day shalt thou be with me in Paradise,' is the whisper of Christ to every saint. They sleep in Jesus, but their souls sleep not. They are before the throne of God, praising Him day and night in His temple, singing Hallelujahs to Him who has washed them from their sins in His blood. It is the body that sleeps so deeply in its lonely bed of earth, beneath the coverlet of grass, with the cold clay for its pillow.

"But what is this sleep? We all know that the surface idea connected with sleep is that of resting. That is undoubtedly just the thought which the Holy Spirit would convey to us. The eyes of the sleeper ache no more with the glare of the light, or rush of tears; his ears are teased no more with the noise of strife, or the murmur of suffering; his hand is no more weakened by long protracted effort and painful weariness; his feet are no more blistered with journeying to and fro along the rugged road; there is rest for aching heads, and strained muscles, and over-taxed nerves, and loosened joints, and panting lungs, and heavy hearts, in the sweet repose of sleep. On yonder couch the laborer shakes off his toil, the merchant his care, the humanitarian his anxiety, the thinker his difficulties, the sufferer his pains. Sleep makes each night a Sabbath

for the day. Sleep shuts the door of the
soul and bids all intruders tarry for a while,
that the royal life within may enter into its
summer garden of ease. From the sweat
of his throbbing brow man is delivered by
sleep, and the thorn and the thistle of the
wide world's curse cease to tear his flesh.

" Just so is it with the body of the redeemed, while it sleeps in the tomb. The
weary are at rest, the servant is as much
at ease as the master or the mistress. The
galley-slave no more tugs the oar, the
bondman forgets the whip, the tempted
one is freed from the tempter, the slave of
the cup is at liberty, no more the worker
leans on his spade, no more the good Samaritan weeps over the ingratitude and
fall of him whose salvation has been his
solicitude. The wheel stands still, the
shuttle is not in motion ; the hand which
turned the one, and the fingers which
threw the other are alike quiet. The long
day, a holiday from the cares, perplexities
and worry of business, has come. The
body finds the tomb a couch for refreshing
rest. The coffin shuts out all disturbance

or effort. The toil-worn believer quietly
sleeps, as does the child weary with its
play when it shuts its eyes and slumbers
on its mother's breast.

"Oh! happy they who 'die in the Lord!'
'They rest from their labors, and their
works do follow them.'

"We would not shun toil, but would
earn our living by the sweat of the brow.
We would not hide ourselves from the fret
and worry of life, for there is no crown of
value without the cross. And yet toil for
toil's sake we would not choose, and when
God's work is done we are so glad to
think that our work is done too.

"The mighty husbandman, when we
have fulfilled our day, shall bid His servants
rest upon the best of beds, for the clods
of the valley shall be sweet to them—for
Jesus is there. Their repose shall never
be broken until He shall rouse them to
give them their reward. Guarded by
angel watchers, curtained by eternal
mysteries, resting on the lap of mother
earth, ye shall sleep on, ye heritors of

glory, till the fulness of the time shall bring you the fulness of redemption.

"But yet once more:—Sleep has its intent and purpose. We do not close our eyes without aim, or open them without benefit. The old cauldron of Medea has its full meaning in sleep. In the old tradition we read of Medea, the enchantress, casting the limbs of old men into her cauldron that they might come forth young again. Sleep does all this in its fashion. We are old enough oftentimes, after hours of thinking and labor, but we sleep and we wake refreshed, as though we were beginning a new life. The sun begins a new day when he rises from the eastern sea, and we begin a new life of renewed vigor when we rise from the couch of quiet slumber.

"'Tir'd nature's sweet restorer, balmy sleep.'

"Now, just such is the effect of the body's visit to the grave. The righteous are placed there, all weary and worn, but such they will not rise. They go there with the furrowed brow, the hollowed

cheek, the wrinkled skin : they shall wake
up in beauty and glory. The old man
totters there leaning on his staff; the
palsied comes there trembling all the way ;
the halt, the lame, the withered, the blind
journey in doleful pilgrimage to the common dormitory, but they shall not rise
decrepid, deformed or diseased, but strong,
vigorous, active, glorious, immortal. The
winter of the grave shall soon give way to
the spring of resurrection and the summer
of glory. Blessed is death, since it answers
all the ends of medicine to this mortal
frame, and, through the Divine Power,
enriches us with the wedding garment of
incorruption.

"One reflection must not escape our
notice—this is not a dreamy slumber. The
sleep of some is much more wearying than
refreshing. Unbidden thoughts steal away
the couch from under them and throw
them on the rack. The involuntary action
of the mind prevents us at times from taking rest in sleep. But not so with the dear
departed. In that sleep of death no dreams
can come, nor do they feel a terror, when

preparing for that bed, for no phantoms, terrors, visions or communications by night shall vex their peace. Their bodies rest in peaceful, profoundest slumber. It is sleep indeed, such as the Lord giveth—' for He giveth His beloved sleep.'

" Nor ought we ever to look upon it as a hopeless sleep. We have seen persons sleep who have been long emaciated by sickness. When we have said ' That eye will never open again : he will sleep himself from time into eternity,' we have felt that the sleep was the prelude of eternal slumber and might probably melt into it. But it is not so here. They sleep a healthy sleep—not thrown over them by death-bearing drugs, nor fell disease. They sleep to wake—to wake in joyful fellowship —to wake when the Redeemer shall come again to claim His own—to awake never to die the second death. Sleep on then, ye servants of the Lord, for if ye sleep, ye shall do well.

"The context, however, gives us a *second* figure. Death is compared to a sowing. The black mould has been plowed ; certain dry-looking seeds are put into a basket, and the husbandman takes his walk, and with hands he scatters right and left, broadcast, his handfuls of seed. Where have they gone? They have fallen into the crevices of the earth; the clods will soon be raked over them and they will disappear.

"Just so is it with us. Our bodies are like the dry grains of wheat. There is nothing very comely in a grain of wheat, nor yet in our bodies. Indeed Paul calls them 'these vile bodies.' Death comes: we call him a reaper—mind I call him a sower—and he takes these bodies of ours and he sows us broadcast in the ground. Go to the cemetery and see his fields; mark how thickly he has sown his furrows; how closely he has drilled his rows; what narrow head-lands he has left! We say they are there *buried*. I say they are *sown*. They are dead, say we. No, say I, they are put into the earth, but they shall not abide there forever. In one sense, these holy bodies of the just *are* dead. 'For that which thou sowest is not quickened

except it die;' but it is not a death unto
death, but rather a death leading unto life.
That mouldering body is no more dead,
than yonder decaying seed which shall
soon spring up again, and thou shalt see a
harvest. We do lose sight, it is true, of
those who have gone from us, for there
must be a burial, how else can the seed
grow? Truly it is never a pleasant sound,
that rattle of the clay on the coffin-lid.
'Earth to earth, ashes to ashes, dust to
dust.' Nor to the farmer, for its own sake,
would it be a very pleasant thing to put
his grain into the dull, cold earth; yet no
farmer ever weeps when he sows his seed.
We never hear the husbandman sigh when
he scatters baskets of seed-corn; rather have
we heard them cheerily singing the song
of mirth and anticipating the reapers' joy,
when they have trodden the furrows.

"Have you ever seen them robed in
black and wearing the dull weeds of
mourning, while they tread the brown
ridges of the fertile earth? We grant,
that considered in itself, it were no wise or
gladsome thing to bury precious grain

amid dead clods of earth, but viewed in the light of harvest, since there must be a burial, a rottenness, a decay, these lose all trace of sorrow, and become prophets of joy. The body must become worm's meat. It must crumble back to its former elements; for 'dust thou art and unto dust shalt thou return;' but this is no more a cause of sorrow, for 'in Christ shall all be made alive.'

"After sowing and decay comes an up-rising, and the farmer soon perceives, in a few short weeks, the little green blade, the son of the buried life. So with the dead; there is soon to come, and we know not how soon, the uprising. We shall thus perceive that they are not lost, but only committed to the ground, in readiness for 'the redemption;' put there that our souls may, when reunited, receive them in a better and nobler form.

"My beloved, if such be death, if it be but sowing, let us have done with all faithless, hopeless, graceless sorrow. 'Our beloved family circle has been broken,' say you? Yes, but only broken that it may be re-formed. You have lost a dear friend? Yes, but only lost that friend that you may find him again, and find more than you lost. They are not lost; they are sown; and as 'light is sown for the righteous,' so are the righteous sown for light. The stars are setting here to rise in other skies to set no more. We are quenched like torches, only to be relit with all the brilliancy of the sun.

Oh how blessed is it to have such a hope in Christ. He has died for us to take away death's sting. He dwelt in the once gloomy grave that he might dispel its ancient terror. And has He not risen again that we may see in Him the first fruits of all the dead who fall asleep in Him?

"Blessed prospect! When He comes to earth again 'the dead in Christ shall rise first,' and then the living saints shall be translated to meet Him."

"Oh blissful thought!
My raptured soul would here no longer stay,
But go to Him in all the glories of an endless day,
To sleep and rise and join the blood-bought throng.
All glory to a risen Lord shall now and ever be my
living, grateful song."

17

THE CLOSING SCENE.

" Then came the end.   Thy rest was calm,
The peace of God spread o'er thy brow ;
The lips pressed tight in pain but now
Smiled sweetly, as though dews of balm
From Eden dropped on fevered frame,
And soothed the pang of struggling breath,
And through the brooding gloom of death
Clear gleams of Heaven's own brightness came."

PLUMPTEE.

On Thursday, February 14th, 1889, Mr.
Godwin attended the weekly meeting of
the Godwin Association, as was his wont.
On several previous occasions he had complained of indisposition, but had not allowed
it to interfere with his attendance, or to
lessen his interest in the work of the
" Home." A class of seven were admitted
to the Association by him on this evening,
five of the men being new candidates, two
of them members who, having lapsed,

sought to be re-instated. His words, spoken evidently with intense feeling, will ever be remembered by the large body of men who almost filled the chapel of the institution. As if moved by a presentiment that a separation was near at hand, he said that, from some inscrutable feeling, he addressed the class before him with diffidence, but with deep affection and interest in their welfare—a diffidence which he could not understand and which was totally unlike his usual frame of mind. He ended one of the most remarkable of his many earnest and loving addresses by saying:

"Never did I feel my responsibility to God as I do to-night. I do not intend to give soft names to sin, or to leave any doubt as to the one great remedy for this sin, or any other sin. If I step into the presence of God to-night, I can honestly say I have tried to do my duty, and when we meet, as I trust we shall, before the throne of grace, you will not charge me with having failed in that duty."

After an affectionate greeting to the newly admitted members, and a conversation with his intimate associates in the work of the Home, he passed from its walls, never again, in bodily presence, to brighten it with his loving and encouraging example and precepts, or to inspire it with his energy, devotion and charity.

After his return from business on Friday, February 15th, he was as cheerful and bright as ever and did not complain in any way. At 1 A. M. on Saturday morning he was taken ill with what was thought to be a violent attack of indigestion. This was followed by a congestive chill, and his physician was summoned. By treatment, and the skilful nursing of his wife, he rallied and rested in comfort. In the morning he rose, feeling completely well, as he said, and would have gone to business but for the earnest persuasion of Mrs. Godwin. Through the day he was fairly well, but weak, no alarming symptoms showing

themselves. Again at 1 A. M, on Sunday
morning he told his wife that he felt far
from well. Physicians were sent for immediately. He complained of a feeling of
great depression and pain about the chest
and heart. This passed away and the
doctors asserted that there was no immediate cause for alarm, but his anxious
wife kept awake all night. About 6.30
he again complained of depression, but
in a few minutes seemed to be resting
quietly. At half-past seven Mrs. Godwin
spoke to him and his answer was full
of affection to the faithful partner of his
joys and sorrows. In a few moments
she heard him breathing heavily and, as
she looked, his great soul left its earthly
abode. Quietly, apparently without pain,
as the early morning rays broke over the
city, he fell asleep in Jesus, asleep there
to rest with Him whom he had served so
faithfully, yea to rest until the day dawn
and the shadows flee away. Upon him

had indeed fallen "the peace of God which
passeth all understanding." Well might
his spirit be said to joy as they joy in
harvest, for he had gathered the fruits of
his labors in the vineyard of the Lord.

When the intelligence reached the
"Home," his faithful friend and co-laborer, the Superintendent of the "Home,"
Mr. C. J. Gibbons, hastened to the chamber of mourning, and, at his request, the
family entrusted the remains to the care of
the members of the Godwin Association,
and in the forenoon they were brought to
the "Home" and placed in the Committee
room, which had so often been the scene
of his earnest pleadings for the continu-
ance of the co-operation of his fellow-directors, and of his counsels for the successful
working of the institution which his labors
had raised to such a height of usefulness.

There, like the body of some hero of
the battlefield, or the senate, it was guarded
by loving hearts until Tuesday, February

19th, when, about mid-day, it was borne
to the chapel, in order that all those who
had loved and honored him in life might
take a last farewell.

In accordance with a wish which he had
frequently expressed, all the arrangements
were of the simplest character; but nothing
could restrain the hundreds who poured
through the door from reverently paying
the tribute of their presence, and comfort-
ing their aching hearts, with one more
look at the well-known face, which death
had not deprived of that expression of
loving earnestness which marked it in life.

Men and women of all ranks of life,
from the wealthiest merchant prince in
the land, to the poorest artisan, men of
many nationalities, men of every profession and occupation were there, anxious
to show on that sad day that they had
known, honored, loved, and valued him
who had passed away; and the number
swelled and swelled, until not only the

chapel itself was filled, but all the adjoining rooms, and many had to turn away
with their longing unsatisfied.

There, in the chapel, amid a few marks
of mourning in sombre hangings, before
the vacant President's chair draped in
black, occupied by a simple white cross,
lay the mortal part of Samuel P. Godwin,
peaceful in death, surrounded by the sweet,
white flowers of innocence and purity, ar-
ranged symbolically, to convey the feelings
of the donors. *The cross and crown*, suggestive of the life of the departed one :

> "Take up thy cross and follow Christ,
>   Nor think till death to lay it down ;
> For only he who bears the cross
>   May hope to wear the glorious crown."

He had taken up the cross in his own
life, and made it the one object of his
teaching ; he had taken it up as his only
hope, his only strength, and he had gone
to receive the reward of those who " have
fought a good fight and have kept the

faith," "a crown incorruptible, undefiled, and that fadeth not away." *The chair* and *the cushion*, betokening rest and sleep after the toils of the day. *The broken column*, signifying that he had been cut off by the decree of God before he has realized the great object of his life, in still further enlarging and deepening the work of the Institution to which he had devoted his best days.

Striking, however, as was the stream of those who filed past the coffin, one feature in particular will not soon fade away: the march of the members of the Godwin Association, men of all ranks, all professions and occupations, who had been raised from vice and restored to virtue by the efforts, example, and influence of the man. One by one they paused, "in all the silent manliness of grief," to take a long, loving look at the features so familiar to them.

The beautiful service of the Protestant Episcopal Church was read by the Rev.

G. H. Kinsolving, the Rector of Epiphany Church. During the service, the choir and congregation sang the Hymn,

" Just as I am without one plea,"

and the Hymn,

:   " Jesus lover of my soul ;"

and two solos :

" Flee as a bird,"

and

" Go bury thy sorrows,"

were also sung by a member of the Godwin Association.

The following address was delivered by the Rev. W. D. Roberts, D. D., of the Temple Presbyterian Church, after a few words of warm-hearted sympathy and regret had been spoken by Mr. Kinsolving:

" He who stands before you has but one element of fitness for the sacred privilege of saying a word beside the body of your beloved President. I loved Samuel P. Godwin ; and I reverenced, beyond the possibility of expression, the Christ-like work for God which he did among his fellow men. To an eminent statesman of the last generation was applied the lofty epithet 'Defender of the Constitution.' To him whose body lies before us we can ascribe a higher title and one which Heaven will more fully honor, 'Lover of Humanity'— and keeper of his weaker brother in the great family of mankind.

"Let me not attempt any elaborate eulogy of the consecrated activities to which the love of Christ constrained our brother, and which the Spirit of God enabled him to put so gloriously into daily practice. Such formal address is not needed; the Franklin Home, continuing his work and bearing henceforth, as it ought, his name, shall be his adequate and enduring monument. Our deathless hearts shall always bear the fresh inscription of his character and service to man. And the members of the Godwin Association in their renewed and noble lives shall be his living witnesses. This large company are all gathered about his casket, as your earnest tear-filled eyes betoken, as those who, every one, in some sacred relation of life must call him your soul's benefactor : and we not only reverence the memory of such a Christ-spirited man, who loved his neighbor better than he loved himself—but of one who lifted you and me upward to the throne of God.

"I wish simply to voice certain timely and vital lessons, which those mute lips, made more eloquent by death, are speaking to us.   Listen reverently, and you will hear those lips say :

"*Every God-fearing man is bound to lead a double life : a life for Christ and humanity, as well as for self.*

"Here lies the body of a busy merchant ; but here also lies the body of a busy servant of God—the body of one whose vocation was merchandise, but whose avocation was the salvation of humanity.   Every Christian man is called by the necessities of his practical life to attend to his daily business—but every Christian man is also called to glorify his Lord and Master upon some field of the arena of God's manifold work in this needy world.   The consecrated man of affairs is not required to forsake his

boats and fishing nets utterly, as the minister is, but he is called to the perhaps more
difficult duty of transforming his work into
worship, and of transfusing the Spirit of
Christ into the body of his secular activity.
No man, not even the busiest merchant,
nor the noblest toiler in material realms,
dare live unto himself alone. God shall
ask of every one of us at the gate of eternal destiny, a two-fold question :—' Where
art thou ?' and ' Where is thy brother !'
And he who has never made any honest
attempt to know where his brother is, shall
not know certainly where he himself is.

"Listen again and you shall hear those
mute lips saying: ' *How great the power
of a consecrated Personality !*'

"This building, this system of finely-
running moral machinery, and this well-
organized institution, have not constituted
the Franklin Reformatory Home. The
personality of this great-hearted brother of
the weak, and that of his efficient Superintendent, and of their noble co-workers,
have constituted this home. A building,
an organization, smooth-running machinery

may be necessities, but it is only consecrated *manhood*, acting through these,
which can save men.   The Christ-filled
personality, the magnetic manhood, the
outreaching spirit of brotherhood of Samuel
P. Godwin, call it what you please, which
was daily grasping, leading, lifting up and
keeping his fellow-men upon the 'Rock
that is higher than we,' constituted the
real Franklin Home.   His time, money,
talents, all were given, but his chief factor
for the glory of God was his winning self-
hood.

"So eminent a thinker and advocate of
institutions as John Henry Newman has
reminded us that the great Revolutions
and Reformations of the world have ever
been accomplished by individual men,
rather than by institutions.   My Brother-
men, how sacred is this gift of personality!
and how awful, in the view of that fact, as
this casket reminds us, that for its great
work we have but 'a little gleam between
the two eternities, no sacred chance for
evermore!'   As we gaze upon these consecrated lips, now forever sealed, these

hands forever motionless, this personality henceforth removed from our sphere, may we cry 'Lord Jesus help me while I live to consecrate every power to Thee and to the humanity for whom Thou didst die.' The lesson of the hour is, 'That thou doest, do quickly.'

"Listen again and hear those lips saying: *There is a glorious Immort:lity in Heaven and on earth for the truly consecrated life.'*

"Had Samuel P. Godwin been only a merchant, the newspapers might have required large space to catalogue the material property which he might have accumulated, and there would have gathered here a group, large or small, of business associates, in grave decorum, but tearless, and with no heartstrings broken, to pay a last tribute of respect. But this is a scene of mourning in depth of feeling and width of contact with which no mere merchant' could be honored. And yet this scene is but faintly symbolical of the ever widening circle, down to the last child of the last graduate of the

Home who shall rise up to bless his name. The beloved benefactor, around whose body we are gathered by the hundreds, men, women and children, with bleeding hearts, was more than a man of business; he was a lover of humanity, a follower of the Lamb whithersoever He goeth to seek the lost. Thus much wider, deeper and grander is the influence of the man who lives for others than that of the man of mere self-pursuits. His immortal self has already entered the gates of the City of God; already he has heard the echoing 'welcome and well done!' Already he has been cleansed even of a sinful nature. Henceforth he stands forth, clear and shining, to the smaller circle of those near and dear to his heart, and to all of us in the wider sphere of his friends and acquaintances, as our glorified one. Heaven shall be rich to him in all that fulness which only they who have been wise enough to win souls can know. Already some who are his crown and joy in Christ have greeted him there, as the one who led them to the Redeemer of men. And how many more shall come up, as the years roll on, to call him blessed. So he made Heaven blessed before he himself entered it. And it shall grow richer and richer to him forever. Some men build up fortunes, inaugurate great undertakings, leave splendid material achievements behind them, as fitting monuments when they die. Samuel P. Godwin, as the Spirit's instrument, turned men's feet from the paths of sin, and planted them upon the Rock of Ages, and put the song of Everlasting Joy in their hearts, and the sound of that song shall thrill his own heart, for ever and ever. ' And they that be wise shall shine as the brightness of the firmament, and they that turn many to righteousness, as the stars for ever and ever.'

"Listen once again and you shall hear those lips solemnly say :—*Take up thy Life-work and carry it on to its glorious consummation.*

"By the grace of God there grew in the soil of this man's human life rarer flowers than the red roses of selfish love of his own flesh and blood ; rarer flowers than the yellow roses of a mere passive interest in humanity *en masse.* There grew, Spirit-born, the pure white flower, more immaculate than these by his casket side, of love to his fellow-man's soul. To the cause of rescuing mankind from the slavery of sin and intemperance he gave his all. By the swift sharp stroke of sudden death, he is transferred to a higher work in the universal system of Christ. The worker is blessed, but his work lies broken at our feet. What is our duty in relation to that unfinished work? I have said that great personalities achieve great decisive victories, but let us not forget that we must look to institutions to carry on to their slow consummation great and noble works. Hence Mr. Godwin's zeal to place this Home upon the solid rock of abiding success. His mute lips to-day say with irresistible impressiveness to every officer, graduate, beneficiary and friend of this institution :— 'Stand by the Franklin Home. Do your utmost to make it a great and ever-increasing success.'

These mute lips say to every man who

in any sphere is destroying the humanity which Samuel P. Godwin loved and lived for so heroically :—' Shame on you!   Halt in your evil course !   You who are your brother's destroyer turn from the evil of your ways and become his keeper.'

"These mute lips say to every Christian moralist, and lover of his fellow-men : *' Take up the work of Temperance Reform. Join hands with that company 'of whom the world is not worthy' who are siruggling for sobriety, purity and true manhood.'*

"Our brother's unutterable earnestness and Christ-like self-giving to this cause ought to stir every man with a heart in him, to tireless activity in the campaign between human souls and soul-destroying sin.   The miracle in the Country of the Gadarenes is repeating itself in this grand work.   We are called upon to decide which shall we do—allow the swine of intemperance and its resultant evils to wander in our fair fields, or secure the restoration and redemption of the poor demoniacs of drink.   The issue is clear and sharp—which

do we love more—the apathy of self-satis-
fied, conscienceless inactivity, or the temporal and spiritual safety and salvation of
the on-coming and un-born generations of
Pennsylvania boys?

" Brave and noble man ! who gavest thy
life to the work of rescue, which had not
been necessary had we, thy professed fellow lovers of men, long ago done our full
duty to mankind in the way of prevention.
We, thy brethren in the common cause of
humanity, pledge ourselves by thy speech-
less body to go forward with thy work ;
and we purpose to direct our energies at
the *fountain head* of this iniquity. One
hand shall be given to the work of rescue,
and with the other we shall deal blows for
the wronged women and children's sake at
the forehead of this bold and brutal traffic.

" And these mute lips plead with every
graduate of this Home, saying : '*My
Brother, having done all, stand! stand in
the power of His might. I am gone, but
your Saviour still reigns, still reigns and
still stoops above you. He sympathizes with*

*you in your trials, mourns over your falls,
and rejoices over your victories.'*

"Remember how constant and impressive was our beloved Brother's testimony that only as we stand upon the Rock of Ages are we safe. In every hour of despondency and of despair, in every tempest of temptation, remember that God the Son, whom Samuel P. Godwin loved, is by your side. And when treading alone the weary burning sands of the desert of God's testing, behold in the hour of need words written across the skies : ' To him that overcometh will I grant to sit with me on my throne, even as I also overcame and am set down with my Father on His throne.'

"So shall you by the grace of God, to which your beloved President and friend owed his all, come at last unto the ' realms of everlasting safety ' and so shall we all, one day, soon at the latest, join our loved ones, gone before, in singing : ' Unto Him that loved us and washed us from our sins in His own blood, and hath made us kings and priests unto God and His Father, to him be glory and dominion for ever and ever.   Amen.'"

So far as the "Home" was concerned all was nearly at an end.   As the family had desired that the interment should be as private as possible, provision was only made for the nearest relations and male friends to proceed to the temporary resting place of the body at East Laurel Hill.

At the conclusion of the service, while the last arrangements were made, the members of the Godwin Association passed out and formed a double line through which the coffin was carried from the "Home," where Samuel P. Godwin had labored for nearly seventeen years.

On the Sunday his spirit had joined the army of the Church Triumphant,

> "Where the songs of all the sinless
> Sweep across the jasper sea,"

His body also had now passed away.

The influence of his example of Christian Faith, Hope and Charity will never pass away, but will find its fruition, when at the last great day, steadfast Faith will be lost in sight, patient Hope will be crowned, and human Love will be made perfect in Divine Love.

CONCLUSION.

" Forgotten ?   No, we never do forget :
  We let the years go : wash them clean with tears,
  Leave them to bleach out in the open day,
  Or lock them careful by, like dead friends' clothes,
  Till we shall dare unfold them without pain—
  But we forget not, never can forget."

MULOCK.

It would be of no practical value to place
on record the multitude of communications
which flowed into the Franklin Home, expressing the deep regret with which Mr.
Godwin's death had been heard of by the
many who knew his life and work. It
must suffice to give a letter, selected from
very many, written by a lady who is a
member of a different branch of Christ's
Holy Church to that to which Mr. Godwin belonged.

"PHILADELPHIA, Feb. 18, 1889.

" MR. C. J. GIBBONS.

" MY DEAR SIR : The papers announce the sad intelligence of the death of Mr. Samuel P. Godwin, President of the Franklin Home.

"His loss to his family is irreparable, but their grief is too sacred for comment.

" His loss to the Franklin Home and to Society generally cannot be estimated, as few men had such rare gifts for attracting men and for always elevating those whom he attracted.

" Unselfish and generous, even to prodigality, in the cause of charity, warm-hearted and sympathetic, his hands were ever stretched out to help those who were struggling, especially those who had fallen victims to intemperance. To this class he devoted his life and the Franklin Home is the living evidence of his active charity and arduous labors for his fallen brothers.

"Well may they grieve! they have lost their friend and benefactor.

" To Society generally the loss of such a

man is a great calamity. His broad-minded views, his entire freedom from prejudice, his readiness to clasp the hand of every man, no matter how differing in creed, if he was a follower of Christ and willing to help a fallen brother, could not fail to influence all he met, rousing some to activity in good works, restraining others from opposition to the advancement of right and truth.

"The writer remembers the last time she saw Mr. Godwin in life.

"It was in the Cathedral, where he stopped after the services in his own church were over ; and though differing in many points from those worshipping there, his large and enlightened mind and his reverence for all that was good, no matter where it was found, made him as much at home as in his own church.

"Surely such a man carried a blessing wherever he went—the blessing of a gentle courtesy that was oil on the troubled waters, and brought peace and good will to those who listened to his kindly advice.

"From his upright life and noble heart, which was large enough to embrace the whole world, one can learn the lessons of forbearance and kindness that will soften the asperities of life and bring harmony and love where bitterness and prejudice too often mar the finest character.

"That the work he so loved may go on, and his example be followed in the Home and in the world, is the earnest prayer of one who admired and reverenced Mr. Godwin in life and in death.

"Sincerely,

"———— ————.""

The estimation in which Mr. Godwin's life, character and usefulness were held by his fellow-directors of the Franklin Home finds an expression in the following resolutions passed by their body :

"God, in His infinite wisdom, has taken unto Himself our President, our associate and our friend.

"Strong in charity and strong in faith, full of love of God and love of man, quick to see the right and swift to do the right, his hand ever stretched to lift him who was prone to sin, his heart ever yearning to

soothe the mortal anguish of stricken man,
ever ready to sacrifice self for the better-
ment of his fellow-creatures, SAMUEL P.
GODWIN recalls to us the enunciation of
the Master whom he served : 'Greater
love hath no man than this, that a man lay
down his life for his friend ;' for he, the
embodiment of vigorous Christian manhood, gave the wonderful wealth of mind
and heart and body with which he was
endowed to God's work, and died doing it.

"Looking back to those dark days, when
the continued existence of the Home was
threatened, when its prospects were gloomy
and many of its friends despairing, we know
the sturdy faith that was in him, how he
'beat his rugged path with bleeding feet,'
never wavering, never fainting, upholding
all about him with the contagion of his
great courage and inspiring them with his
splendid energy, and through the rifting
clouds there broke the sunlight of Divine
favor.

"That he lived to see the Home what
he had striven to make it; that he remained
with us until there were garnered fruits of

the seed he had sown, we give gratitude to God.

"We regard him as a man especially suited to his time, his place and the social conditions which appealed to him with such force. It was consonant with the human idea of Divine harmony that he was given to us when he was, and none can say that it is not in consonance with that same Divine harmony that he has been taken away. He had done his work, completed his task, as nearly as any man can. He had made his impress on the world, and such was the permeating character of his influence that he has imbued others with the courage, the confidence, the charity and self-sacrificing disposition which distinguished him.

"In token, therefore, of the esteem in which we held him in life, and the sorrow which, in spite of the knowledge that he has gone to be rewarded by his God, must afflict us in this separation ; be it

"*Resolved*, That in the death of SAMUEL P. GODWIN all human endeavor has lost an ardent promoter, the organizations of

which he was a member have lost a powerful factor in their successful conduct, and
those among whom he moved have lost a
sterling friend. The Franklin Home especially will feel his loss, for to its building
up and to the work to which it was devoted
he gave the vigor of his younger manhood
and the mature judgment and unstinted
aid of his later years.

" *Resolved*, That we offer his family our
sympathy and commend them to the consolation of that God whom he served so
gladly and faithfully, and in whose service
he gave up his life.

"*Resolved*, That this preamble and the
connected resolutions be engrossed and
presented to his family, as a memento
for them of the regard in which the husband and father was held by his fellow-
men."

No one who was present in the Chapel
of the Home on the evening of Monday,
February 18th, 1889, will forget the solemn
silence, the almost hopeless look on every
countenance, the crushed and broken-

hearted feeling which pervaded the very room, as the members of the Godwin Association sat there, awaiting the official announcement which all knew full well must fall from the lips of the Vice President of the Association.

The resolutions passed testify to the feelings of the men who found difficulty in putting into words the sorrow which had eaten its way into their very hearts. They are as follows :

"We, the members of the Godwin Association of the Franklin Home of Philadelphia, assemble together to express and record our sense of the irreparable loss which we have sustained in the death of our President, Mr. Samuel P. Godwin.

" The founder of our body, the guide, counsellor and friend of each and all of us ; he spared no effort to work out the idea which he carried next his heart—the restoration of the erring ones of God's fold to a Father's love and favor by inculcating true repentance ; the securing forgiveness through the Cross of Christ, which he ever held out as the only means of man's salvation ; the implanting of hope in the heart and the strength to walk worthy of our vocation by the grace of that Holy Spirit without which he ever taught that it is impossible to please God.

" We feel that no words of ours can express the affection with which we regarded him, or the esteem with which his self-denying and noble life inspired us.

"We feel that the death which has robbed us of his bodily presence is gain to him, and while we place on our records our heartfelt grief at his departure from among us, we pray that the lessons which he conveyed by example, as well as precept, will lead us all to that rest to which our Father has led him.

"We resolve that in our own lives, by carrying out the grand charity to fallen ones, which he taught and practiced, and to which his life was devoted, we will endeavor, with the help of God, to raise such a monument as he himself would desire, a monument far more enduring than brass or marble.

" We would assert our conviction that his memory will never fade from the hearts of those who have loved and valued him, and would declare it to be our hope that we all may be reunited with him before that throne where ' they who turn many to righteousness shall shine, as the stars, for ever and ever.'

" *Resolved*, That we regard with deep gratitude the consent of Mrs. Godwin that the mortal remains of our late President should be entrusted to the care of the Franklin Home and the Godwin Association, to which he had dedicated his life and work.

" *Resolved*, That a copy of the preamble and resolutions be forwarded to the family of our late lamented President, with an expression of our deep sympathy with them in their hour of sorrow."

Not only at the Franklin Home, and among the members of the Godwin Association was Mr. Godwin's death felt. Temperance Associations through the country knew not only that a powerful advocate of their cause had passed away, but that an eminently practical worker in the difficult sphere of the reformation of the fallen, had ceased from his labors. In the Library of the Home there hangs a framed message of sympathy to the Association from one of the societies of the State of Delaware, a copy of which is here given :

"At a meeting of the YOUNG MEN'S TEMPERANCE UNION, of Wilmington, Del., held at their rooms at No. 800 Market St., February 25th, 1889, the following Preamble and Resolutions were unanimously adopted :

"WHEREAS, We have learned with feelings of the profoundest sorrow and regret of the death of Samuel P. Godwin, late President of the Godwin Association of Philadelphia, our friend and co-laborer in the cause of temperance and morality ;

"WHEREAS, Through all his life and services there has shone the lustre of a

gifted and noble manhood, and of a disinterested devotion to grand ends and aims.
A safe counsellor, a true Christian man, a
philanthropist and friend has gone to his
reward. The influence of the words and
acts of such a man will outlast the bronze
and marble fashioned to make his name
immortal. There is a fragrance and a
perfume that lingers and floats back to us
from beyond the dark River of Death,·
which he has so peacefully crossed. His
name and memory are dear to us. He
has left the community the legacy of a
well-spent life. We revere his memory
because the beneficent influence of his life
has given us confidence in the present and
hope for the future. The sunlight of his
life has faded away, but the bright guiding
star of his example remains fixed in the
firmament. Though death has deprived
the cause of Temperance of his services,
and us of his friendship and support, it
cannot take away the grand results of his
untiring labor.

" *Therefore, be it Resolved,* That we, as
friends and brothers in the cause of Tem-

perance, express our deep and heartfelt regret at his death, and the consequent loss to the cause of humanity and morality, of one of its most ardent and powerful supporters.

" *Resolved*, That we tender to the wife and kindred of the deceased the assurance of our sympathy in their sad bereavement.

" *Resolved*, That as a fitting tribute to the memory of Samuel P. Godwin, these resolutions be suitably engrossed and presented to the Godwin Association of the Franklin Reformatory Home of Philadelphia, of which he was President and founder ; that they be entered upon the minutes of the Young Men's Temperance Union, and that we drape our headquarters in mourning for thirty days.

HARRY E. DOLLOW,
Chairman.
MAHLON H. HILLES.
W. C. PAWLEY,
President."

One other testimony must suffice and it was given by the one who has labored so faithfully and earnestly for nearly seventeen years in furthering Mr. Godwin's plans and carrying out his ideas, the Superintendent of the Franklin Home, Mr. C. J. Gibbons.

On Sunday evening, April 7th, 1889 a service was held in the Chapel of the Home to celebrate the seventeenth anniversary of the commencement of Religious Services in the institution. Among the addresses delivered was the following one in which the bosom friend and fellow laborer spoke of his dead leader and comrade :

"Under the Providence of God, it has been my privilege, my dear brothers, to celebrate with you Seventeen Anniversaries of the commencement of Religious Services in the Franklin Home.

"It is with no ordinary feelings of gratitude that I join you in praising and thanking God for His goodness in protecting and guiding us through all these years, years that have been marked by successes and reverses, by health and sickness, by evidences of the noblest and most self-sacrificing friendships, and by the basest deceits ; and yet through all, by the blessing of God, I have been enabled to fight on and upward, so that to-night, fullying realizing the consoling words of St. Paul, I can say that ' I am what I am, by the grace of God '

" But the thanksgiving we feel to-night is overshadowed with sadness for the loss of our friend and benefactor, the lamented Samuel P. Godwin, the President, and, one may truly say, the corner-stone of the great work to which he devoted the best years of life and died laboring to perfect it.

" To-night our hearts yearn for his genial smile, the warm grasp of his hand and the tender sympathy he had for all, especially those who were struggling to reach a better life. We miss his sound advice, the fearless and bold enunciation of truth, in which there were no weak or hesitating lines, no false sentiment, no glossing over of evil to suit the views either of society or of the individual.

" Yes, we indeed miss the founder, the

builder of this grand work, the man who has stamped so indelibly the impress of his own character upon it, that it became the noblest and most enduring monument of his life and labors.

" But if we miss our beloved President to-night, a Christian's Faith and a Christian's Hope enable us to realize that our loss is his gain, and that God knew what was best. He has taken him from a world of care and sorrow to receive the blessed reward promised to those who do their Master's will.

"Speaking thus in reverential memory of our departed friend, I would call your attention to the present condition of the Home.

"There have been three important events in the history of the Franklin Home.

" The first was its birth, when the philanthropic thoughts of a few humane men, seeking to save a fallen brother, passed from mere philanthropic thought into Christian action, bringing into existence a charity that is unique in its character and far-reaching in its labors—an Ark floating

on the waters of sin and sorrow, that
affords shelter and protection to the un-
happy men whom the storm of temptation
is hurrying to destruction. That Ark is
the Franklin Home.

" At the earliest period of its life, through
the providence of God, Mr. Samuel P.
Godwin was called to be its overseer.
Under him, to use one of his favorite expressions, the battle was bravely fought
and gloriously won, which made this Home
the Christian Home that it is, instead of a
hospital, or a mere lodging house, where
men could straighten up after a debauch,
and build up and rest to prepare for another spree.

" God and the wisdom of its founders
brought it safely through its first great
danger and planted it firmly on a secure
foundation.

" The second event was in 1880, when
the Home received a blow, so terrible and
so unexpected, that consternation filled all
hearts. But the same honest, earnest men,
who had called this grand work into being,

now stood around it, determined at every sacrifice to save it.

"The Board of Directors met, prayer to God was offered in this time of sore trial, and again did God carry us safely through the dark waters, giving us new life and hope ; and the work thus blessed went on more prosperously than before, for experience, though a stern, is yet a thorough teacher.

"But the hardest blow fell in 1889, on the Home and on us all. The Home lost by death its revered President, we lost a tender father, and humanity lost a friend. His work, however, goes on, his spirit still lives, because his teachings were of 'Christ crucified' and His power to save.

"Dark and hopeless were those three days in February, which followed his death. Human nature sank beneath the crushing blow, but we were awakened by the memory of his teaching that 'all things work together for good to those that love God,' and as the echoes of his words came rushing in upon us, we said, though feebly, 'not our will, but thine be done, O Lord.'

" We felt then the great responsibility which rests upon it, and felt, too, that the highest eulogy we could pay our beloved friend was to carry out his teaching in our lives.

" To-night, while standing within the shadow of his vacant chair, I feel that I can say for you, my Brothers, what I can say for myself, that this work will go on year by year, unfolding new beauties and fresh fruit, until we too are ready to be gathered into the everlasting home, where we shall join him we love so well, when the re-claimed and the reclaimer will meet at that bar of God he so often spoke of, and where we shall rejoice together in everlasting joy."

Here now must end the account of the life-work of one who, among the circle of his relatives and friends, was valued as a good man, who devoted his life to deeds of charity.   To them belongs

> " That best portion of a good man's life,
>   His little, nameless, unremembered acts
>   Of kindness and of love."

The Godwin Association of the Frank-

lin Home yield not even to that circle of
friends in the love for him as a *good* man,
but looking round, as they do weekly, on
that Home organized and developed by
him, they would humbly say, " He was a
great man." Lowly as the violets of early
spring, he shed his sweetness on the air
around him, and now that " the Reaper—
Death"—has gathered him with the " sickle
keen," no word of murmuring may cross
the lips of those who have to walk in his
footsteps until they too are called hence
to join him.

Rather let all say :

> " They who die in Christ are bless'd ;
>   Ours be then no thought of grieving ;
> Sweetly with their God they rest,
>   All their toils and troubles leaving :
> So be ours the Faith that saveth,
> Hope that every trial braveth,
> Love that to the end endureth,
> And, through Christ, the crown secureth."

And now abideth Faith, Hope, Charity
these three, but the greatest of thes'
Charity.